Praise for Sean Murphy's
THE HOPE VALLEY HUBCAP KING

"It isn't often that I get that delicious tremor of
anticipation when I begin to read an unknown
book. Samuel Beckett, I venture to say, would gladly lay
claim to this rich, vast, and slyly
comedic novel . . . you may have regrets in your life, but
reading *Hubcap King* will not be among
them. Read and rejoice."
—Malachy McCourt

"Ingenious and exhilarating . . . this book has 'future cult
classic' written all over it!"
—*Publishers Weekly*

"The adventure is a social commentary, amusing but also
profound . . . a lively, thought-
provoking road trip to enlightenment."
—*The Santa Fe New Mexican*

"A funky comic novel . . . The spiritual aspects of
this book are sometimes subtle and poignant,
sometimes silly and irreverent, but always rich in
meaning . . . a wild adventure."
—*ld-Sun*

Also by Sean Murphy

THE HOPE VALLEY HUBCAP KING

ONE BIRD, ONE STONE:
108 AMERICAN ZEN STORIES

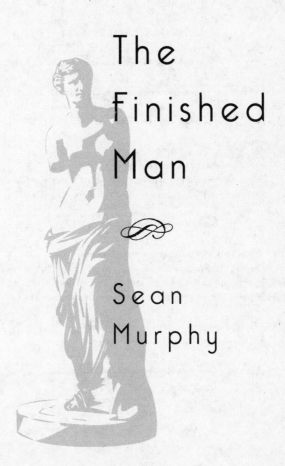

The
Finished
Man

Sean
Murphy

DELTA TRADE PAPERBACKS

THE FINISHED MAN
A Delta Book / February 2004

Published by Bantam Dell
A Division of Random House, Inc.
New York, New York

Book design by Lynn Newmark

Library of Congress Cataloging-in-Publication Data
Murphy, Sean.
The finished man / Sean Murphy.
p.   cm.
ISBN 0-553-38244-6
I. Title.

PS3613.U755F56 2004
813'.6—dc22   2003055826

Manufactured in the United States of America
Published simultaneously in Canada

10   9   8   7   6   5   4   3   2   1
BVG

For Tania

Acknowledgments

This book would not exist without the influence of my grandmother, Marie White, who provided my earliest coherent childhood memory, and the notion of the Finished Man. She is sorely missed, as is my aunt Dorothy White, whose guidance, wisdom, and encouragement were pivotal in my life, and whose sense of humor and unconventional approach to living provided inspiration for many scenes in the book. Thanks too go to Donald Fagen for taking care of Dorothy and for helping introduce me to the world of "Malomar." Particular appreciation goes to Fiona Thompson and Mirabai Starr, who read the manuscript and contributed invaluable advice throughout its development, and especially to Fiona for inventing a number of the best titles for Max's "100 Types." Thanks always to my intrepid editor Liz Scheier for shepherding the book through its conception, labor, and eventual (sometimes difficult!) delivery, and to my agent Peter Rubie for handling the business with his usual flawless panache.

Finally and most important, boundless appreciation to my wonderful wife, Tania, to whom this book is dedicated, and without whose love, inspiration, emotional support, and ceaseless editorial suggestions, it just wouldn't have been very good.

The
Finished
Man

I

In Which I Renew an Old Acquaintance

I'D BEEN successfully putting off my goal of becoming the greatest living American novelist for nearly ten years, when I ran into my old classmate Max Peterson on the Malomar Pier one afternoon, looking out to sea. He had a cigar that must have been a foot long stuffed between his jaws, smoke billowing from its end like the stack on a freighter, and the ocean beneath him was cresting up in blue wedges, as though the sky had fallen at his feet and was all bent out of shape.

The way he stood there, tall and broad, legs like an A-frame against the railing, it looked as though he'd brought the sky down on purpose, by sheer will, and now loomed over it, head and shoulders above the ragged procession of fishermen and tourists on the pier, as though he were master of the world. As he turned away from the rail I recognized

the permanent, slightly superior half-smile on his blocky
features that had made him so unpopular at college. But his
illusion of invincibility was broken by the weight he'd gained
since our last meeting and the new deep lines drawn in his
face. For a moment I saw him as pure geometry, a walking
Picasso: squared-off head and chest over that round, almost
spherical paunch, a circular bald spot at the apex of his scalp
topping it off.

I'd heard that Max was in Los Angeles, but I'd hoped, if
truth be known, to avoid seeing him during my stay. In our
graduate writing program at Boscoe, Max had earned the
reputation for being a bit of a jerk: supercilious, contentious,
uniformly scathing in his response to work he considered in-
ferior—in other words, anything produced by anyone but
himself. Meanwhile, everyone I knew considered his writing
to be nothing more than a heap of pretentious scribblings.
But he'd had a certain confidence, even then, that made him
somehow charismatic, so you couldn't help liking him, or at
least being fascinated in the midst of your dislike. Maybe it
was his big, sad eyes, like those of a dog or a pony, that made
it seem as though he'd suffered, as though he'd somehow
earned the right to his misplaced arrogance.

I remember he once told a group of us at school, during a
discussion on favorite books and authors: "*I only read my
own work.*"

But legends had adhered to Max that hinted there was
more to him than we could see. It was said he'd spent a
summer traveling across Canada in a car with no engine—a
near-miracle achieved by repeatedly flagging down passing

motorists and asking them to tow him to the next town. Once, it was reported, he was accused of shoplifting in a department store, and he'd stripped himself naked on the spot to demonstrate his innocence. And his sexual achievements, if one believed the rumors, were nothing short of remarkable.

A few years back he'd received considerable acclaim for a best-selling novel titled—and I wince to repeat this—*City of Breasts*. I'd never owned a copy, but I picked it up from a friend's bookshelf while house-sitting and, with a kind of repulsed fascination, read it through to the end. The opening went like this:

> The building's dome thrust up through the haze of the city like an enormous bosom. Smog clung in gauzy strips, like nylon stockings, to the hills. The sun sent shafts of light shimmering between the clefts of the skyscrapers. The curves of the Hollywood Freeway below me were enormous, mammarian. Blond starlets cruised by in low-cut sports cars.
>
> Ah, I thought to myself, looking down upon it all. Los Angeles: City of Breasts.

The story, such as it was, detailed the obsession of a man much like Max for a woman he believed to be the most beautiful in the world. The heroine was a thinly disguised version of another of our classmates, Magee.

Ah, Magee.

I'll never forget the first time I saw her. It was during a party at the home of one of my more progressive professors, shortly after I'd arrived at Boscoe. I heard music coming from upstairs and, feeling out of place, as I generally did at such gatherings, made my way up to investigate. There was a knot of onlookers, mostly men, gathered around a doorway at the top, from which emanated music of such passion and intensity that the very air seemed to vibrate with emotion. I shouldered my way in and there she was: sitting before our professor's baby grand, auburn hair tumbled across her face, fingers cascading across the keys, entirely lost in sound. There was no sheet music visible, and she played with her eyes closed; a scotch wobbled in its glass and a cigarette burned in an ashtray. I later discovered the music was Chopin: but the performance was all Magee.

She finished and, paying no attention to her onlookers, tossed back her hair and reached for her drink. She stubbed out her spent cigarette, shook a fresh one from a crumpled pack of Chesterfields and lit it, exhaling a cumulus of smoke into the room. *Self-pollution,* I thought with the attitude that was my customary stance at the time; I was a near-teetotaler in those years and had never smoked a cigarette in my life. But her music had no trace of impurity. And Magee herself seemed to exude an extraordinary vitality—a light nothing could dim.

Magee soon transferred to the writing program, where I, along with the rest of my male classmates, spent the next years dreaming of becoming her lover. But whenever the crowd went one way, I went the other. I made it my business to avoid her and her ever-present horde of hangers-on. This, to her credit, provoked in her a certain fondness for my company; and so we became friends after all.

But friendship with Magee, I soon discovered, was a subtle and exquisite form of torture—not because she encouraged my feelings for her, but because she did nothing of the sort. Magee was a passive goddess: if men sacrificed themselves to her, they did it of their own volition. And so after graduation I'd drifted out of contact. Still, in all the years since, I'd never managed to overcome my dreams of one day becoming worthy enough to win her.

Max, meanwhile, sold his next three books, as yet unwritten, for six figures each.

All of them were optioned by Hollywood.

He married Magee.

I should have refused to have a drink with him that afternoon, purely on principle. But as I was about to slip away from the pier unseen, he spotted me. "Frankie, my boy," he called. "Frank!" The fact that he'd always called me "Frankie, my boy" or even "Frankie, my lad" was one of the reasons I'd never liked him. That, and his habit of standing too close during conversations—as he proceeded to do a moment later, tilting over me and puffing cigar smoke like a human volcano. As we spoke I noticed he'd missed some spots shaving; stiff bristles teetered in the canyons of his face. His breath smelled of cigars and Jack Daniel's. He summarized his recent successes, tut-tutted me over my unfinished novel, clapped me on the back a dozen times too many.

Now, I like to tell the truth whenever I can; an out-and-out liar always offends me. And the only thing I hate more than a liar is a sneak. Max had always struck me as both. He was a braggart, arrogant, brash—too full of himself, too full of everything, like a balloon about to burst. I don't know why I went with him that afternoon. If I'd stayed behind and watched the old men fish, as I'd planned, everything would have turned out differently.

2

In Which I Am Led into Adventure
Against My Will

I GET these feelings. Call them intuition, call them whatever you like; but I know when something good is going to happen, and when something bad is going to happen. And when Max took me by the arm that afternoon and marched me down to his car to join him for a drink, I knew right away this was going to be bad.

So what does it matter if I don't like him? I reasoned. *What's the harm in just having a drink with the guy?* After all, it was possible that he'd changed. It had been ten years.

But I think I knew even then that the reason I was going along with it was that I wanted to see Magee again, no matter the price.

"How about we head down to San Melonica?" Max suggested. "The Frantic Pelican. My favorite dive." Max released my arm and clicked a button on his key ring; a blue Ocelot

8 Sean Murphy

Z-6000 in the lot before us let out a toot of a horn and flapped the lids on its headlights coquettishly. I slid into the leather passenger seat like a hand slipping into a glove. Max shut his door and exhaled a last cloud of acrid smoke into the interior. He mashed out his cigar in the ashtray and lit a cigarette, then switched on the air-conditioning and pulled out onto the Coast Highway. I found the button and rolled down the window on my side an inch or so to let some air in, but Max caught on and rolled it up again.

"These twelve-cylinder models can't handle open windows with the AC on." He puffed a billow of smoke in my direction. "They just overheat." He put the pedal down and sped off into the traffic. I could feel the engine throbbing up through the floorboards like some great trapped beast.

The highway was jammed up at Sunrise as usual and we must've sat for ten minutes before we could get through the light. Max shrugged. "Saturday afternoon. What can you do?" He lit another cigarette. The car in front of us had a couple of bright yellow surfboards strapped to the roof. The vehicle on the left had a board sticking out the back window, fin poking up like the back of a shark. On the right was an old Mustang convertible filled with happy-looking young people wearing no shirts, and yet another surfboard nosing skyward from the backseat. Near as I could tell, we were the only vehicle without one. Being fresh from the East Coast, and not fully acquainted with local customs, I wondered whether this might be grounds for a driving citation.

We pulled away and I glimpsed, through the belching exhausts and the smoke haze inside the car, the distant outline of Catatonia Island across the blue expanse of the Pacific. For Southern California, this qualified as a clear day.

As we ascended the incline to San Melonica I could see rising before us a pair of odd cantaloupe-shaped concrete balls topping the pillars that marked the entrance to the town.

"See?" winked Max. "City of Breasts. What'd I tell you?"

We had one Jack Daniel's, and then another; then I nursed a beer while Max had several more. The Frantic Pelican featured a nautical motif, with crossed sets of oars over the bar and an entire lifeboat hanging from the ceiling. Netting and buoys drooped low overhead. Between the bluish light and the currents of smoke coasting about, it was a lot like being underwater. Max and I talked over the old days at Boscoe, then moved on to writing in general and the purpose of art: things writers discuss when they don't have anything else to talk about. Or at least writers who have MFA degrees do— which Max, Magee, and I all had. Major Fucking Achievement, Max always said it stood for.

Max looked every bit the successful author, wearing a black turtleneck beneath his obligatory writer's corduroy jacket—although he'd acquired a new affectation since I'd last seen him: a white silk scarf, with tasseled ends, draped casually about his neck. A Hollywood thing, I supposed.

Finally I couldn't avoid asking how his sequel to *City of*

Breasts was going. It had been two years since the first novel had been published, and all that had come out in the meantime was a volume of short stories, most of which I remembered from college.

"I'm just about finished, my boy. It's coming out this fall."

"What are you going to call it?"

He paused for effect. *"The Telltale Breast."*

"'Telltale *Breast*?'" I repeated. "Oh Max, you can't do that, can you?"

"Can and will." Max leaned back in his seat, grinning, and clipped the end off one of his enormous stogies. They were so big I wondered if he'd had them specially made. "Want one?" He gestured toward me with a leather cigar case. It looked like it was made of snakeskin or lizard—some hapless reptile that didn't deserve to have died for the cause. I shook my head.

"Don't smoke? I'd forgotten." He lifted an eyebrow and looked at me with his sad gaze as though this was some kind of personal disappointment. Then he shrugged and lit up, using an old-style silver lighter. "Well, far be it from me to lead you astray." He puffed away with vigor, the end of his cigar glowing like a warning beacon through the hazy air.

You might suppose, given Max's writing style, that the critics weren't likely to be on his side. But to my amazement, some of the younger ones had recently picked up on his work. They praised him for his passion, for what one called his "accidental originality." One pointed to his symbolic use of recurring breast motifs; another praised his use of menstrual blood as foreshadowing. No less an authority than August Snipe, of the *LA Times,* had hailed Max's work as the creation of a new wave in fiction, for which he'd coined the phrase "Punk Schlock."

In an admiring review of Max's story collection, *Beverly's Hills,* Snipe had written: "These tales are so dark you can scarcely see the words upon the page."

As far as these pundits were concerned, the more pulpish and mercenary Max's books were, the more they succeeded in being the perfect reflection of America.

Other observers were not so appreciative. **SCHLOCK TACTICS** read the headline in the *Scranton Review.* **CLICHÉ AWAY** said the *Newark Times.*

"It just kills me," Max was saying. "To think of it, my books selling like hotcakes all across the country. And as good as they are, you gotta know some critic's gonna pick them up who just hates them. These people drive me crazy!"

I had to admire him, if only for his pure, thickheaded cluelessness. The point was, he didn't know he was writing trash. He thought he was the greatest thing since Shakespeare.

Max leaned in again, too close. "Listen, you're my old school buddy. I think I can let you in on the secret of my success, can't I?" He looked at me with one eyebrow raised and one lowered, in what I supposed was intended to be a significant glance.

"Sure, Max," I shrugged.

He stage-whispered: "It's the research."

"Research?" I couldn't figure out where he was going with this. After all, *City of Breasts* could hardly be called a scholarly piece of work.

"Yep." He blew a fresh blast of smoke in my direction and examined the end of his cigar. "It's all about the research." With that he proceeded to reveal more than I would ever want to know about his private life. It seems that at some point during his sexually stultified adolescence he'd conceived an aspiration that would set the course of his life to the present day: he would make love to one example of every type of woman in existence. In recent years he'd narrowed down the task to what he called "The One Hundred Fundamental Varieties of Women."

The worst thing was, he was serious about it.

"Max"—I couldn't think of anything else to say—"this sounds like Heinz ketchup or something. Are there really only one hundred varieties?"

"I'm talking basic types. There are variations, of course, and perhaps in the future I'll have a chance to check them all out. After my retirement, maybe." He grinned. "But for right now, I'm working through my list."

"Your *list?*" I was about to say more, maybe to protest, I don't know. But the concept was so mind-boggling it erased every conceivable response from my brain cells.

"Listen, Frankie." Max looked at me with an earnestness that, despite myself, I found almost endearing. "There are no frontiers left. There are no heroes anymore. Love is the only adventure in the modern world."

"But, Max—"

"No buts about it, my boy. Look at the animals. Origin of the species, survival of the fittest—all that. If it does not fuck, Frank, it does not exist."

I didn't know what to say to that.

"Frankie, my boy," Max's voice took on an intimate tone, and his eyes welled up as though in concern. And the funny thing was—for you could never pin Max down, or anticipate what was coming next—the concern seemed genuine. "Frankie," he asked, "when was the last time you were *with* a woman?"

"I, well . . ." I was about to bluster a false reply: "Friday," or even "last night." But somehow those eyes drew me in. They were just so big and sad I couldn't tell a lie before them. "To be honest"—I glanced down at my watch to check the date—"it's been three years last Thursday."

"Frankie," Max shook his head sadly. "You've always been a little too—how can I say this—restrained in your approach to sex. You need to loosen up, buddy! Listen to your old pal."

I listened. I didn't have much choice at that point. We'd come in his car, after all, and I didn't have the money for a cab. And in Los Angeles there's no other way to get home.

"Just think of it, Frank. Consider the possibilities: Dark-haired debutantes from Atlanta with voices sweet as peaches and a mint julep in each hand. Coffee-skinned Creole women from New Orleans with café au lait complexions and hair piled up on their heads like the whole thing's ready to blow. Busty, recently graduated cheerleaders from Dallas with thighs like ice cream and fifty-three different fight songs imprinted in their tiny memories. Brown-eyed girls from the barrio who dance salsa with you all night and eat your heart for breakfast . . ."

I couldn't stand it anymore. It all sounded rehearsed, as though he'd repeated these lines again and again to himself in secret, countless times over the years. And he probably had. "Thighs like ice cream?" I protested. "Isn't that a mixed metaphor or something? I mean, I just don't think it works."

Max grinned, sat back, and worked at his cigar for a while. I was squirming in my seat. The chairs had those semi-circular arms that came around like someone embracing you from behind, and wooden seats designed to dig into your bottom in the world's most uncomfortable way. Maybe, I thought, this was a means of encouraging you to buy more drink to ease the pain. I kept glancing at the lifeboat above our heads, wondering if the ropes were going to hold.

"But, Max—" I managed to get out. "What about Magee?"

"What about her?" The gaze on that blocky face was per-fectly smooth, inscrutable.

"Is she faithful to you?"

"How should I know?"

"But"—I sputtered—"doesn't all this mean you have to *lie* to her?"

He burst out laughing. "Ah, Frankie, it's just telling an-other story. That's my business. If we don't have stories, what have we got? Chaos! One thing happens, then another, and another after that—it's all so tiresome." He took a big swallow of his Jack Daniel's. "It's all fictions, see?" Max was trotting out one of his favorite theories from the Boscoe days. "We're all creating fictions. I don't mean only us writers. I mean preachers, politicians, businessmen, schoolteachers—the whole world."

"Still, how can you——"

"Listen, kid." Max looked at me, lips clasped around his dwindling cigar butt that was beginning to look more and more like a smoldering dog turd. "Just because a guy's married doesn't mean he has to give up his life's purpose." He took the cigar from his mouth and leaned in on me again; for a minute I thought he was actually going to put his arm around my shoulders. "These things are different for a man. I mean, consider the Virgin Mary. Think of the respect she gets. But you never hear a thing about the Virgin Joseph. All those years he never got any, but does Joseph get any credit? No. Mary gets the glory. He's just poor old Joe, who never got laid." Max rolled his cigar over in his mouth, crunched down on it. "I'll tell you one thing. These women can play the Virgin Mary all they want. But I'm not gonna be no Virgin Joe."

Yep, I thought to myself. *Max is still a jerk.* But I couldn't help admiring him in some strange way. After all, I thought, wasn't being a jerk better than being just another nobody— another boob in front of a television set, not even good enough to be a jerk?

We were about to go. The room had started to swim—or should I say I was beginning to feel like I was swimming through it, that whole hazy tangle of nets and buoys and ships' propellers. Max had already paid the check, eyeing the petite blond waitress up and down. ("Hey, Max," she'd flirted when she'd set our drinks down, and afterward I'd seen her whispering with the bartender, beneath the crossed oars, casting glances in our direction. "Already checked that one off the list," Max had winked. "Number 37, Bar-room Bombshell . . .")

I'd begun the daunting process of getting to my feet when Max grabbed my arm and tugged me back into the seat beside him.

"Frankie, my boy—" His brown animal eyes looked bigger and fuller than ever. "Can I ask you a question?"

I settled back into the wooden seat, feeling the sore spot on my rear from the whole afternoon of sitting there. Max leaned forward as though he were about to divulge the most intimate information yet in this already too-intimate encounter.

"Frankie, do you think that *writing*—I'm not talking about just *any* writing, I'm talking about *my* writing—do you think it's useful?"

"Useful?" I said. "It brings in a paycheck, doesn't it?"

"What I mean is"—he came in closer, so I could smell his breath, smoky and bitter, see his pupils dilated and dancing in the shadows—"do you think it does anybody any good?"

"Ah," I said. "The big question."

"The biggest." Max nodded solemnly.

I couldn't resist. After all, we were talking honestly, weren't we? "Well," I shrugged, "I doubt it."

For a moment his features hardened. He pulled back and

I could see that big, squarish frame stiffen beneath his jacket. But all at once he laughed, and clapped me on the back for what must have been the fortieth time. "Ah, Frankie, you always did tell it to me straight, didn't you?" He chuckled. "You know what? I doubt it too."

By the time we got out of there I was thoroughly seasick, and Max was practically staggering. The sun was about to set, and he insisted on taking me for a walk around the neighborhood—which was fine with me, as I wasn't eager to see what effect his condition might exert on his driving skills. We stumbled around for fifteen minutes or so, then took a turn onto Venison Boulevard, with its traffic and rows of shops. Max paused, swaying a bit, in front of a store called The Happy Booker.

I don't know if I can do justice to the shop's sign. It was designed to look like a movie poster, featuring a blond starlet-type in a low-cut pink dress. She had an open book where her breasts should have been, with strangely rounded covers. It was the only book I've ever seen with cleavage.

"This isn't a bad place—" Max began, pointing at the window, but then stopped in mid-sentence. "Hey!" he said. "Hey!"

"What?" I could see several copies of *City of Breasts* showcased behind the glass. "That's pretty good placement, Max."

"Placement?" he sputtered. "They're supposed to have the *new* edition in the window. The one with the Hollywood Book Awards emblem on it. Hey!" He rapped on the window at the proprietor, a burly, balding fellow who'd just finished turning the sign around to read CLOSED and was now cashing out the register. "Hey!" Max rapped again.

The sun had gone down, though there was still a reddish wash over the sky. Streetlamps were coming on up and down the boulevard.

"Relax," I said. "You can call him in the morning."

"Now," he cried. "I have to deal with this now!" Max just strode over to the door and knocked again, but the owner just pointed mutely to the sign, then turned back to the register. "Don't you know who I am?" Max was banging on the glass now with the flat of his hand.

"Chill out," I said, taking him by the shoulder. "We can take care of this tomorrow."

Jesus. I was already saying *we*.

He shrugged off my hand, turning to look at me. His face was flushed and sweat was coming out above his eyebrows. "Doesn't he know who I am? My picture's right on the back cover!"

"Max—" I began, but he turned back just as the proprietor, with an impassive gaze, pulled down a shade from above the door, closing us out.

Max stood there. For an instant I thought he was going to cry.

"The bastard! I'll show the bastard!" He pounded on the glass. "I'm the author of the goddamned book!"

"Listen—"

Max stepped back and looked about wildly, eyes as wide

and unfocused as a deer caught in headlights. They settled on a trash can filled with bottles waiting on the curb to be taken to recycling. Before I could stop him, he sprang into motion like a moving, sweating mountain. "The bastard!" With a kind of hysterical strength, Max lifted the can in a single motion and hurled it against the window.

The glass shattered, broke, went everywhere, just like in the movies. A wailing siren shrieked into action and lights began to flash. Max turned to me with panic on his features, as though he'd woken from a dream and had no idea where he was.

"What do we do now?" he asked.

"Run, you idiot!" I grabbed him by his coat and shook him once, hard. "Run!"

I turned and did exactly that, practically dragging him along behind me as the owner burst onto the sidewalk after us.

"You mothers," the man was shouting. "I'll get you for this!"

Max's feet finally connected with his brain. We ducked along an alley, Max's scarf twisting wildly behind him as he ran. We scrambled over a fence, then dropped to the top of a Dumpster, cut down a couple of side streets and across a parking lot, and came up to the Ocelot the back way. Max surrendered the keys without resistance. I loaded him into the passenger seat, climbed behind the wheel, and screeched out of there. For a long time he didn't say anything, just sat in the seat with his coat rumpled and his hands clasped in his lap like a child, rocking back and forth. Then he started to laugh in a strange, high-pitched squeal I hadn't heard before.

"I thought that son of a bitch had a gun," he said, still rocking. "He was so mad I thought the bastard was gonna shoot us!" He began to laugh harder, almost uncontrollably. Then I began to laugh too as we dropped down the incline to the Coast Highway.

"Frankie, my boy," Max was almost choking. "You sure got me out of that one!" He clapped me on the shoulder. "I owe you one, buddy. I owe you one."

We sped down the darkening highway, laughing together.

Man, that Ocelot sure had some power.

3

In Which I Have Too Much to Drink and Discover What Drives the Whole Universe

TWO NIGHTS later the phone rang at 3:00 A.M. "Frankie, my lad," the voice came over the receiver, jubilant and slurred. "It's me, Max."

I suppressed the urge to say something about his identity being obvious.

"Max," I said, "do you know what time it is?"

"Of course, Frank. It's Now. It's always Now! Frankie, we're having a party tomorrow night. We want you to come."

"What's the occasion?" Given the hour, and the fact that I was standing barefoot in my aunt's kitchen in my tattered old bathrobe, I couldn't think of anything else to say.

"Friday the thirteenth. We always have a party on Friday the thirteenth. We're famous for these things. Everyone's coming. Hey, we want you to get over here early so we have a chance to visit. Magee wants to see you."

"But how am I going to get there?" I was living at my aunt's house in Trillion Oaks, on the other side of the Coast Range from Malomar. In Los Angeles terms, this was equivalent to living in Antarctica. I borrowed her old Buick for my basic needs, but I was pretty sure she wasn't going to be keen on me taking it so early in the day and being gone, presumably, till after midnight.

"We'll come over in the Ocelot, get you at ten in the morning."

"Ten A.M.? Max, are you out of your skull?"

"Has there ever been any doubt? Hey, see ya in the morning, buddy. Oh, and bring some things with you. You'll be spending the night." The receiver clicked down.

This was the summer of the great drought in Southern California, and my life had gone dry, dry, dry—dry as the tawny brown hills that lay between my aunt's house and the still-green strip of Malomar beside the ocean.

The other night Max and I had driven together back to Trillion Oaks; then Max, against my advice, had made his own way home in the Ocelot. So I'd never gotten to see his place. I figured what the hell.

Besides, I thought, this might be the only chance I'd get to see Magee.

It was after 11:00 the next morning when a taxi, inhabited by a lone, grumbling cabbie, showed up in our driveway. I kissed my aunt Clara good-bye, promised her I'd be careful, and made my way down the walk with my overnight bag, packed with too many clothes and my disheveled manuscript that accompanied me everywhere, despite the fact that I hadn't looked at it in weeks. I figured I might find a chance to work on it if I got bored at the party, as I generally did. I'd always felt out of place at these kinds of things: gatherings, events, jobs, life. My existence often seemed less like living than like watching life in a mirror, where I had to do everything backward to get it right.

It was the same unfinished manuscript that had provoked my aunt to offer her spare bedroom for nine months, rent-free. *After all,* she'd said in her letter, *that's how long it takes to make a baby. And if you can't finish it in that time, you're not going to finish it at all!* I'd felt inspired enough to fly out from the East Coast five months ago to take her up on it.

"Get it out of your system," my uncle Charlie had said, taking his leave of me at the airport. "Come back, nine months, the family business is waiting for you."

He owned a chain of dry-cleaning establishments in Newark, where I'd spent the most spiritually annihilating childhood known to humankind.

"After all," he'd clapped me on the back, "you *are* my brother's son. Flesh of my blood, blood of my flesh, and all that."

I'd always hated being clapped on the back.

After graduating from Boscoe I'd kicked around, taking odd jobs, working off and on at my novel. When people asked what I did for a living I told them: "I borrow." If they inquired further, I explained that since nature abhorred a vacuum, I'd made it my mission to create a money vacuum in my life, in hopes that the universe might feel compelled to fill it. Thus far, I had to admit, it hadn't worked.

When they asked what the novel was about I'd answer: "You." That generally shut them up. But I'd been bogged down now for several months and didn't even know what the story was about anymore. I spent most of my time alone in my room at my aunt's house, reading Tolstoy and tracts on Buddhism.

Although I didn't realize it at the time, I was shortly to find my true subject, in Max and Magee.

We took the sinuous route through Malomar Canyon, cliffs rising sheer and unclimbable to the right, plummeting hundreds of feet to the river bottom on the left. "A lot like life," I remarked to the cabbie, who didn't seem inclined to philosophize. We made the left onto the Coast Highway near Saltspray University, then down the hill and in past the Enclave Market onto Old Malomar Road, hidden behind a steep ridge that seemed to fall straight from highway to sea, so you'd never know the neighborhood was there. The cabdriver pulled up to a gate and punched in some numbers. "You know the code?" I asked.

He shrugged. "I pick up a pizza or something for them at least once a week."

I'd recognized the house from below based on Max's description. Perched uneasily at the top of a winding driveway on a hillside overlooking the coast, the place was a sprawling pink stucco monstrosity with actual turrets that might best be described as a castle. ("A man's home is his castle," I would often hear Max quip in months to come, showing it off to visitors. "Yes," Magee would respond wryly, "and his car is his penis.")

The structure was set into the face of an uncomfortably steep slope, in a way calculated to make Easterners like me nervous; but for Malomar this was nothing out of the ordinary. As Max himself said: "Better make sure the place is watertight, 'cause if the Big One comes, we're headed out to sea."

Still, for all the talk about the "Big One" in California, I never met anyone who seemed to believe it could actually happen.

I could see Max's squared-off frame standing at the top of the drive as we wound our way up the hill. Silhouetted against the sky, he looked larger than life, as though he were Paul Bunyan, some mythical child's figure assembled out of blocks—although in this case an enormous cigar substituted for the customary lumberjack's ax.

Max paid the cabbie. I thought I saw fifty dollars change hands—enough to keep me in groceries for a week. Then, as I stepped out from the back, to my utter amazement, Max plucked his cigar from his mouth and kissed me smack-dab on the lips. "Ah Frankie," he said, throwing an arm around my shoulders as he led me up to the house. "It's great to see you. You really got me out of a fix the other night, didn't you? So what do you think of my place?"

We stepped together into the front room: and there she was. If life had a sound track, it was time to bring on a crescendo.

Magee, bright-eyed and dreamy, sat against a sunlit, bougainvillea-draped window with a pen in her hand and a notebook in her lap. Cigarette smoke coiled bluishly above her head. She looked like a painting, I thought, haloed in light with the riot of flowers behind her; some nineteenth-century scene by a French master. She glanced up casually, as though she'd just seen me last week, then rose to take my hand.

"I dreamed of horses last night, Frank. I was just writing it down." It seemed an odd way to greet me after ten years, but that was always Magee: poetry before propriety. "They were the most beautiful things, a tawny bone color, sleek and elongated——like greyhound horses, if that makes any sense. They were running free on the beach, but you could ride them if you could catch one. They were wearing these beautiful hand-tooled Spanish saddles, and their necks were long and stretched forward like gazelles. They dashed up and down the beach together like a single great animal. . . ."

"Why don't we get you a horse," suggested Max. "You could have one, you know. We have the space."

"Oh no," said Magee. "I couldn't bear to have anything so . . . dependent on me." She gazed off for a moment, then turned abruptly. "Oh, but Frank, how *are* you? I haven't seen you in a million years." She gave me a hug and a kiss on the cheek, the hand holding the cigarette draped over my left shoulder. Then she stepped back to look me over.

Those million years had treated her well. She looked incredible. Her dark, almost black hair swept to her shoulders in a kind of a Cleopatra cut, with bangs along her forehead. She'd had light brown hair the last time I saw her, but that was no matter—she was always changing something about herself, one way or another. She wore a bright yellow sundress, beneath which the collection of curves that was her body moved, shifted, breathed. Her tanned calves were bare and she had no shoes on. Her eyes were that same oceanic green they'd always been: sealike, I thought to myself not for the first time. No islands in those eyes. They were eyes on which, once set adrift, you could float for centuries. The ash on her cigarette had grown long while she was talking, and I watched with a kind of fascination as, when she went to take another drag, it dropped to the floor. No one seemed to notice.

"I dream a lot these days," she said to me, exhaling smoke over my head. "I've been keeping track of them. A couple of nights ago I dreamed Rapunzel got a perm, so when she went to let her hair down it wasn't long enough anymore. . . . And the whole story never happened. She never got saved."

They showed me around; I won't go too much into the details, but it wasn't exactly my kind of place. The furnishings appeared to be a compromise between the two of them: glass-and-chrome coffee and end tables (Max), potted palms, ferns, and spider plants (Magee); a state-of-the-art TV and video system (both of them). The flooring consisted of large blocks of expensive-looking tile partially covered with throw rugs; an enormous picture window peered out over the coast. But the most striking feature was the mirrors. The front entry and the wall around the stone fireplace in the living room were both

mirrored from floor to ceiling. Antique mirrors, many of
them in gilt frames—a recent obsession of Max's—hung on
the walls where you'd expect to find paintings. Even the light
switches were mirrored. Everywhere you went in that house,
you were looking at yourself. The one peculiar note was
Magee's old brown felt sofa from Boscoe, which she'd refused
to part with. It looked as warm and saggy and comfortable as
ever, if a bit out of place in the glossy environment of the living room.

The gardens, admittedly, were beautiful, draped in
bougainvillea and wild rose—"lovely, but full of thorns," said
Magee. A fountain featured a stone replica of the Venus de
Milo with water spurting from her nipples, given to Max by
his publisher at Triple Knight Books after *City of Breasts* hit
the best-seller list.

"We wanted to make it squirt milk," explained Max, "but
we couldn't figure out how to keep it from going sour."

I stood with them on the stone patio, gazing at the expan-
sive views of the Pacific coastline, buried in haze. The rain
forests in Mexico were burning that summer—they were
having the worst drought in a hundred years, and every time
the wind blew from the south the smoke swept up and engulfed the entire region.

"It's so parched this season." Magee glanced up at the
steep expanse of browning grass above the house and parking area. "There are wildfires everywhere. We live in fear."
She smiled, incongruously. Her voice lilted, like water
falling on stone; and I couldn't help but wonder whether

fear, or anything like it, was something she or Max had ever really experienced.

They introduced me to their maid, Lupe—"Loopy, I call her," put in Max, brightly—and her sister Esperanza, who helped out when needed. "Her name means Hope," Magee explained. "Isn't that lovely?" And they pointed out their gardener/handyman working on the far side of the patio, whose name, Magee said, was pronounced "Hey-soos," although it was spelled "Jesus."

"Hey—Dr. Seuss," Max quipped to him with a grin, at which the gardener, toiling over the ground, merely lifted his hand and gave us a little wave.

"Imagine," said Magee, "if we named ourselves like they do. What would we be called? Inspiration? Zoroaster?"

Then there were the dogs, two enormous bull mastiffs that Max had insisted on adopting over Magee's protests. They were named, in keeping with their tremendous, primeval vitality, Alpha and Omega. They'd been locked in their kennel for my arrival.

"They're very sweet really, once they get to know you," said Magee. "Their bark is worse than their bite."

A good thing, too, I found myself thinking a moment after they'd been released: for their bark was pretty fearsome. They circled, yelping and bounding, for several minutes while Max and Magee tried to get it into the beasts' walnut-size brains that I was a friend. Then, abruptly, they settled down; and as we continued our tour of the grounds, I felt a wet, sloppy tongue against my dangling hand, and looked down to see one of them—Alpha or Omega, I could never be sure—grinning up at me, I swear.

"They're not very smart, I'm afraid," Max warned. "You have to keep an eye on them all the time. They'll just go after anything they want without thinking about it."

The castle had a ballroom which, bizarrely, doubled as a makeshift basketball court, with baskets mounted beneath the high ceilings, above the doors at either end.

"Care for a game of hoops?" Max asked. "We have time for a quick one before they set up for the party. Just watch out for the chandeliers."

Surprisingly, although he insisted on lighting up a cigar that he somehow continued to successfully smoke while playing, Max was very good. He had a magician's touch with long shots, jump shots, even wild hooks from center court. And he could dribble like nobody's business. Inside fifteen minutes he had me beaten eleven to three.

The parquet floor was covered with ashes and burn marks.

Afterward Max showed me up to the guest room. Occupying the westernmost turret of the building, it featured vertiginous views of the coastline to the south, and the ocean several hundred feet below. Predictably, the decor consisted almost entirely of mirrors. A Victorian looking glass with a wooden frame occupied one corner; a mirrored rectangle dominated the space above the dresser; a spotty, ancient-looking oval hung against the closet door. After Max left I stood there for a long time, lost in a crowd composed entirely of myself. There I was, all around me, everywhere I looked: average height, average build, sandy hair of average length, a bit disheveled; blue Levi's and gray Boscoe T-shirt, black Converse high-tops. The most thoroughly average-looking fellow I could imagine. What on earth was I doing in Malomar?

Following an afternoon break, which I used to catch up on last night's lost sleep rather than working on my manuscript as planned, I decided to take a walk along a stretch of relatively flat, open hillside that spread north from Max and Magee's property line. The browning fields stretched unbroken, not another house in sight. The dogs caught enthusiastically on to the enterprise and bounded ahead. I made my way along the vacant land, populated with anise and pampas grass and—oddly—several patches of bird-of-paradise plants, as though there had once been a garden here. Although they looked a bit dry, I figured they must get enough moisture here beside the sea, perhaps from the morning mist, to survive.

The sun was beginning to set. There was a bruised spot in the sky over Los Angeles. To the south I could dimly see the dark arm of the Polo Vandale Peninsula sweeping down through the smog into the ocean. I was thinking about Magee. She still had something, all right. Something that, at age thirty-three, the years had not erased—as if, I reflected, they would dare. But what *was* it? It was a sort of fire, it seemed: a brightness that, despite the constant haze of cigarette smoke that surrounded her, she'd always emanated. She was beautiful, certainly. But the world, and Los Angeles in particular, was filled with beautiful women. It was something more than that. She was, I decided in that moment, a peculiarly unique and special brand of being: a being of light.

The dogs had gone off somewhere up the hill; I heard them thrashing about the patches of pampas grass, occasionally emitting a short, sharp bark. Before me rose a small, inviting-looking grove of eucalyptus trees; as I approached more closely I could see a series of odd dark patches on their trunks. Behind was a large rectangle of blackened earth, surrounded by a rim of what appeared to be crumbled concrete blocks.

It suddenly came to me: *there's been a fire here.*

Prowling among the piles of blackened bits, I spotted the gleam of something half-buried but still shining. Taking the splintered end of a roofing board, I dug through the rubble until I'd unearthed it: a grotesque melange of melted silverware, fused together by heat. As I stood there, holding it in my hands, brushing off the ash, one of the dogs—Alpha or Omega, I couldn't be sure which—came bounding up with great excitement and laid something at my feet.

It was the head of a rabbit, whole and entire.

Magee had gotten into the habit of throwing formal dress parties; and to my surprise, here in Southern California, where people show up to the fanciest restaurants clad in T-shirts, she had succeeded in getting everyone to go along with the idea. So when the gathering started to get off the ground, right around dusk, I felt like I was in another era, something out of *The Great Gatsby*. She'd had Lupe and Esperanza working all afternoon with three assistants, a florist, and a caterer; the place was decked out with flowers and candles and colored streamers and looked terrific. Strands of lights snaked around pillars and twinkled amidst the bougainvillea; Chinese lanterns shone beneath the eaves; a life-size swan carved out of ice glittered and sweated at the center of the patio. There was one eccentric touch: in the ballroom, now laid with banquet tables and a buffet, the basketball hoops were still in place. No one seemed to notice.

Magee had arranged a rental tux for me. As I watched the fine automobiles pull one after another to the top of the driveway, Saabs and Mercedes and BMWs, I kept sliding my finger between my Adam's apple and the silly bow tie that felt like it was choking me. What good were ties, I couldn't help wondering, when they had no purpose except to cut off our wind? *Nooses,* I thought, *we all had nooses looped around our necks and not one of us realized it.*

It was that time of evening I love best, when the sky turns turquoise along the western rim, seeming to melt straight into the ocean. A full moon had been ordered up for the occasion, and I was standing in the garden, watching it rise over the eastern hills, when I heard a voice behind me.

"It's a long way from Boscoe, no?" It was Magee. She had a yellow flower behind one ear, and her hair was all braided up in one of those French-Italian-type dos. She'd done something to it, I don't know what, but it wasn't just dark anymore; it had glinting red highlights all through it. It was as though she had flames in her hair.

I could hardly speak before the spectacle. "What's that flower?" I finally managed to get out.

She was wearing a long white old-fashioned gown, a lacy thing with a low-cut front that showed off her cleavage to magnificent effect. A slim gold chain nestled above her collarbones. With the wreaths of smoke swirling about from her freshly lit cigarette, she looked like some sort of fire spirit that had just descended out of the clouds. I wondered whether she had set the whole party up like this, with everyone wearing black, so she could be the only one in white.

"It's a dahlia," she smiled and drawled at me, breathing out smoke, "daaahhling." She took my arm and strolled me along the patio. "Frank, you look fantastic. Very distinguished in that tux. Now I want you to tell me everything that's happened to you in the past ten years. Love life?"

"Well, actually, no, I don't lately," I tried to quip.

My summary of the prior decade took all of three minutes, after which Magee walked me around and pointed out the various guests. "There's the singer Mocha Brown. She's terrific. Oh, and those are the film commentators Flak and Shrapnel. That guy over there's a producer; he's got the *Hip Hazard Private Eye* show and *Slowly but Shirley,* and that program about the twins, *Tom and Tom Again.* See that couple?" She pointed to an elderly man doddering along with a cane, accompanied by a flaxen-haired woman who might have been his granddaughter. "She married him for his money. It's the blonde leading the blind." She grinned at me with her head cocked to the side, exhaled a cloud of smoke, and looked back over the crowd. "Those two men over there are terrible writers. Max calls them the illegible bachelors. Oh, and that's the actress Page Turner. I once heard someone call her terminally relaxed. She leaves chocolate on the other side of the bedroom every night so she has a reason to get up in the morning. And that guy, I don't remember his name, but he's a famous scatologist, wrote a book called *The Origin of the Feces*."

I'd been letting it all go by right enough, but now I looked at her. For a moment she kept her face straight, then dissolved into laughter.

"Did you just make all that up?" I didn't have a TV, hadn't been to a movie in months, so she could've said anything and I'd have believed her.

"I'm not going to answer that." She averted her gaze in mock shyness and flapped her eyelashes. But all of a sudden her face turned serious.

"I'm actually terribly bored with all this," she said.

"I don't blame you." We stood there looking at each other. Then, all of a sudden, I don't know why but I was struck by something—or rather, the absence of something that would never be lacking out in the country at this time of year back East. Here we were, outside at dusk in the early summer, and—

"Hey," I said. "How come there aren't any mosquitoes?"

"We don't allow them in California," said Magee. "It's against the law."

I walked off by myself, thinking it over. Magee was brighter than Max, funnier, more talented. And too beautiful

for him. Entirely out of his league, actually. What on earth
were they doing together?

I spotted Max's blocky form amidst a circle of tuxedoed men,
all of them smoking the same foot-long cigars. For once, I
thought, Max wouldn't be able to stand too close to these people, for fear they'd all catch fire. His paunch was sticking out,
and as he glanced around, inspecting the crowd and puffing his
cigar, he looked like nothing so much as a self-satisfied busi-
nessman. I overheard him describing his new book as I walked
by: "It's a sort of homoerotic CIA drug thriller from the other
side of the Hollywood tracks. . . ."

Whatever *that* meant, I thought. But at that moment he
spotted me.

"Hey, Frankie, I've been looking for you. . . . I wanted to
show you something." He excused himself from the group and
walked me up the hill to where a double garage stood above the
parking area, close to the dog kennels. Although I'd noticed the
structure before, for the first time I realized it had a second
level—perhaps an apartment for live-in help. Its windows
were uncurtained, throwing rectangular snippets of darkening
sky, like movie frames, back to our eyes. Max opened a side
door and flipped on a switch; a dim, bare bulb came on overhead, revealing a vehicle draped in a grayish dust cover. Max
paused long enough to deliver one of his trademark significant
glances, one eyebrow up and one down. Then, like a game-
show host unveiling a grand prize, he drew the cover aside.

"Wow, Max," I exclaimed in honest astonishment. "You've still got it?"

It was the Trojan Hearse, his legendary trysting machine from our college days.

"A hearse, a hearse, my kingdom for a hearse!" Max cried, reprising his famous partying slogan.

A secondhand funeral limo he'd bought from a mortuary near Boscoe, it had been outfitted by Max with a bed in the back; it already had curtains and everything else he needed—although it had taken weeks of airing before he could rid it of the scent of formaldehyde.

"It's in incredible shape." I ran my finger over the still-glossy black paint job and the gilt emblems on the side. "Do you drive it?"

"Not much," he said. "Magee hates it, of course. Runs fine, though. Every once in a while I take it out for a spin." He looked over the machine, patted it fondly on the flank. "Yep, I must've scored a couple dozen items off my list in this thing: #17, Well-Endowed Farm Girl; #21, Rebellious Heiress; #24, Seattle Grunge Gal . . ."

Items? I winced to myself. But all I said was: "At this rate you must nearly be through your Hundred Varieties."

"Yeah," he mused, "you'd think so, if only some of them weren't so hard to come by." He grew reflective. "Sometimes I'm at a loss as to how to proceed, except to go over old ground again. You know, it's a bit like taking classes back at Boscoe. Sometimes you have to repeat them to make sure you've got it right."

38   Sean Murphy

"What's on the other side?" I asked, indicating the partition that separated the garage into halves.

"It's Magee's old Mercedes. Here, I'll show you." We moved through to the other side and Max switched on the light to reveal a gorgeous contraption with rounded fenders and running boards and a wooden dash that must have dated from the 1950's.

"She doesn't use it much, I'm afraid," Max said. "Little things are always going wrong, and it's tough to get parts. Right now it needs a carburetor—guess we'll have to order one from Germany. But Magee doesn't get out too often anyway. We mostly just share the Ocelot."

The sky was violet-gray over the ocean by the time we stepped back outside; night crept stealthily across the ridge behind us. As we stood there I saw the first star appear overhead, as though it had been created that moment.

"You know what, Frankie?" Max said. "I think I'm gonna get me a helicopter. Learn to be a pilot. We could put a landing pad right here on this roof!" He sucked pensively on his cigar. "I've been thinking I ought to have some sort of hobby. Take my mind off my work."

"Maybe you should get a mistress," I suggested, but either he didn't hear me or didn't realize it was a joke.

"Then again," he mused, "I do love driving that Ocelot. Maybe I should get into racing." All of a sudden he pulled the cigar from his mouth, as though he'd just discovered it sitting there. He looked upon it with disgust. "You know what?" he said, "I'm sick of these things. Starting tomorrow, I'm going to stop smoking and drinking. Work off this gut. I figure it's never too late to get in shape!" With that he put the cigar in place again and began puffing away happily, as though the idea was all that was needed to bring contentment.

After that it was time to hit the buffet. I ended up with a full plate before me in the ballroom, on a surface I recognized from lunch as Max and Magee's own dining-room table— moved in here, perhaps, because they'd come up short on seating. There had been no real guest list, after all, and no one had seemed to have any idea how many people might show up. The table was a fancy hardwood piece, now draped in a white cloth, and they'd brought out the four matching chairs that had worked fine with it this afternoon. But the extra folding chairs that came with the caterer weren't high enough, so when I sat down the tabletop came nearly up to my chin. I felt like a child eating with the adults, having received the admonition to be seen and not heard.

The food was that "fusion cuisine" stuff: green-chile poppy-seed nori rolls and quinoa croquettes with mango chutney, that sort of thing. I'd worked up an appetite, what with all the running around after Max and Magee and the dogs, and I dove right into it—although it wasn't a very long dive, the plate being only a couple of inches below my face. It was several minutes before I came up for air and bothered to look around at my tablemates.

Down at the end was the man Magee had identified as the scatologist, although I felt too self-conscious to ask if that was what he really did for a living. He was holding forth, however, as though he was an expert on something—religion, perhaps—despite the fact that he'd gotten stuck with one of the small chairs too, and his head barely cleared the edge of the table. I found out later that he was a professor from over at Saltspray, by the name of Vern Akler.

"It's relatively common," he was saying, "for travelers to Jerusalem to be seized by the delusion that they are the Messiah, even if they have no prior history of mental instability. There are therapists in Israel who specialize in treating this type of disorder."

I don't drink much, and I was feeling a bit tipsy already, and perhaps that's why I found myself zoning out on his words and focusing so much on his face. Or maybe it was because that was all I could see of him down at the far end of the table, looking for all the world as though he was no more than a head propped up there, talking away all by itself.

His features struck me as archetypal. He had a nose that seemed to me the very essence of noseness—as though if one were to look up *nose* in the dictionary it would be his that was illustrated in the margin. He had a mouth that could only be termed eminently oral, its wide aperture lined with teeth that hung down in perfect stalactitinous order. And his eyes were ovals of sublime perfection. He looked like a living, breathing piece of statuary, a marble bust from antiquity.

"Some Talmudic texts," he continued, "assert that twenty-six failed attempts preceded the final, successful Genesis."

Yes, I couldn't help thinking, and apparently some of them had resulted in the creation of sentient, speaking heads with no bodies.

A phrase from the next table cut in, like another channel interfering in a radio transmission. It was a woman's voice, high and grating: "My obsessions appear to be progressing phonetically. At this point, it's Jung and Yoga——"

"To be followed, perhaps," responded a man's voice, "by Zebras and Xeroxing?" Laughter.

"I have it on good evidence," Akler was saying, "from numerous Old Testament sources, that there were only a few thousand souls in the original creation at Sinai, and no new ones created afterward. Ever since, apparently, they've been splitting them up between us."

The rest of our table's inhabitants looked on with expressions ranging from interest to indifference. Half of them looked like big kids, faces hanging in their soup. The only one actively participating in the conversation was a man who seemed to speak entirely in interjections—or maybe it was just that Akler never let him get a word in edgewise. Every once in a while the fellow would spit out something like: "Ah, hmph, er, harrumph . . ." but other than that the professor held the stage.

"Who's 'they'?" spoke up a brave individual at last. I'd noticed him trying to get a word out for a while, but he was hampered by the fact that, being even shorter than the rest of us, his eyes barely cleared the tabletop. I later found out this was the actor Huffy Dustbin. Even if I would have recognized him, however, I never *could* have, as I had only half his face to go by. Maybe that's why he was attracting so little attention from the other guests.

"What?" Akler paused for a moment.

"Who's 'they'? The ones who are splitting up the souls?"

I couldn't blame Akler for not being able to hear.

Dustbin's mouth, after all, was under the table. But the attempt, although it went unanswered, created the first real opening in the conversation.

"So we've each only got a fraction of a soul?" put in an ethereal-looking blond woman, the only one present aside from Magee who was wearing white.

"Doesn't that seem obvious?" said Akler. "One doesn't have to go too far back into history to realize that all the great human beings were the ones who lived before. Odysseus, Agamemnon . . ."

"Helen of Troy?" Magee sauntered up, choosing an utterly appropriate moment to break into the conversation.

The professor hemmed and hawed. "Well, you can hardly put Helen of Troy in the same category as——"

"But we have to include the women, don't we?"

That, remarkably, shut him up for a while.

I looked around. I was into my fourth glass of champagne. The place was packed. If there were only a few thousand souls at Sinai, I thought fuzzily, a good percentage of them must be here. Not to mention a high proportion of Max's Basic Types. I wondered if the woman at the table, Ethereal Blond Actress with Philosophical Leanings, was on his list.

But now Magee was speaking, and there wasn't an eye at the table that wasn't upon her. "I suppose I might be able to believe in one of those *ancient* gods," she said, lighting up a fresh cigarette, "if they still had some power. Zeus, or Thor. Quetzalcoatl—now, there's a god for you!" She exhaled a white cone of smoke.

"Ah, but here we are in the Golden West," put in the ethereal woman, provoking an up-and-down glance from Magee. "We are living a myth, are we not?"

I was feeling more than a little out of my element. I glanced up at the basketball hoops, which still didn't seem to be attracting any attention. For some reason this gave me satisfaction.

Eventually the talk turned, as it always did in California during the dry season, to fire. The ethereal woman had been through the Doppleganger Canyon blaze the year before. She told tales of people barely managing to get out of their driveways, tires burning off their wheels as the flames roared down the canyon with 60-mph Santa Ana winds behind them. She knew people, she said, who had been burned out of their homes three times, who had not a single photo left from their childhoods.

Meanwhile, the interjection guy was continuing to carry on a conversation, of sorts, with the philosopher:

"*The Iliad* being the best record we have of the . . ."

"Er . . . hmm. Oh?"

"Cultural development of ancient . . ."

"Uh . . . aarrgh. O.K.!"

"City states in the Mediterranean . . ."

"Give him an inch," remarked Magee, nodding toward Akler, "and he'll talk a while."

A jazz quartet was starting up. They were playing "Give Me a Ghost of a Chance."

I'm not sure what happened next. All I know is that I found myself standing in what appeared to be the living room, talking to a woman I couldn't recall meeting. Someone had lit the fire-place, and the room felt hot: too hot for this time of year. The woman was the author of a popular feminist tract titled *Of Mice and Menstruation*. She was telling me about her new project, which, she explained, dealt with deconstructivist theory as applied to postmodern culture, her particular focus being rap music. But all *I* could focus on was the fact that, lodged between her right cuspid and the adjacent bicuspid, there was a bit of seaweed from one of the postmodern nori rolls, which deconstructed her smile every time her lips parted.

"So you see, when the rapper Poodle Spot Poodle talks about 'packing a piece' . . ."

That piece was really packed in there. That little chunk of seaweed so dominated my attention that I lost track of what she was saying and sank into a sort of trance, watching it appear and disappear from behind her lips, and longing with an almost sensual desire to reach over and pluck it out.

What kept me from mentioning it? If I had a piece of nori roll between my teeth, I was sure I'd prefer to be told about it, instead of carrying on an entire conversation without ever being heard. At least, I *thought* I would. Or would I rather just continue in ignorance and spare everyone the embarrassment?

But then, drinking always makes me philosophical—one of the reasons those close to me generally discourage me from doing it. I started picking at my teeth with the fingernail of my right pinky, hoping that might inspire her to action.

"Consider Stallion," she was going on. "Examine his *Rhomboid* films from a deconstructivist perspective and you'll find . . ."

How many things were like this? I wondered. How many situations where we'd rather coast along in ignorance than face the truth? She'd gone through the entire interaction never dreaming I'd hardly heard a word she'd said, all because of a bit of aquatic greenery that couldn't have been a centimeter across.

It's the small things, I reflected, that come between us.

I watched, as though from a distance, as she took her leave and crossed the room to talk with someone else. I wondered how often she'd repeat that experience. Perhaps for the entire evening. Maybe she'd go home and brush her teeth and never realize the seaweed had been there at all, and merely be left with the lingering feeling that nobody ever listened to her. Maybe she'd make some decision based on that feeling—leaving her husband, getting another job—that would influence her entire existence.

Wasn't that just like life?

I wandered into the night to take some air, and took another champagne from a passing tray, which was probably a bad idea. I felt as though I was made of glass, as though if I bumped into someone the wrong way, I just might break. I wondered if Max and Magee could see into me, examine my small intestine, my gallbladder, my spleen. I wondered if everyone could.

The party was moving onto the patio, where Lupe and Esperanza had lit candles and tiki torches: a questionable choice of decor, I thought, given the drought conditions. The quartet had just launched into "Beneath the Fool Moon." People stood in knots and clusters, lit by the flickering glow, doing things with their mouths: drinking, smoking, talking:

"Oooh, have you seen Bobby Zipperman? Everyone keeps saying he might be coming tonight. Don't you just love his new album?"

"And over there, is that Sexton Tarantula?"

"Tarantella," corrected someone. "He's very fussy about the pronunciation."

"Check it out, isn't that Rochelle Piper?"

I was surrounded by people talking about other people. It all seemed so—I don't know—incestuous. Every movement seemed choreographed. Everyone looked brand-new, as though they'd sprung out of clay that afternoon.

A group of women was clustered by the Venus statue, discussing certain individuals who'd clearly been behaving abominably. So-and-so had left so-and-so because he'd slept with so-and-so, who was *really* married to so-and-so, who actually turned out to be so-and-so's brother.

"Who *are* these people?" I couldn't resist breaking into the conversation.

A silence fell over the group. "What planet have *you* been living on?" someone said. "They're characters from *Generally Inhospitable.*"

I wandered past Magee, who was in the midst of a conversation about the current trend for models and actresses to have no cleavage. "Yes," Magee was saying, "that's a great worry to Max, since we all know that's his area of specialty. . . ."

Appreciative laughter from her listeners.

She held court, serene and inviolate, like some kind of icon, the founder of a new religion. In another time and place, I thought, she and Max would have been royalty. Fallen royalty, perhaps, but royalty. If not king and queen, then duke and duchess at least. Magee: Duchess of Malomar. It had kind of a ring to it, I thought.

"The latest trend is to have no hips, either," someone put in.

"Yes," said Magee, who lacked neither of the attributes in question. "I hear they're having them surgically altered. It's called hip-o-suction."

Magee was a flame, I thought, and there must have been a dozen admirers whirling about her in confusion. Some of them, particularly a corpulent movie producer she'd been steadfastly repelling all evening, appeared to be singeing their wings in the process.

Max, meanwhile, was having a literary conversation at the opposite edge of the patio.

"In the beginning was the Word, was it not?" I could see the glint of his teeth, the glowing tip of his cigar circling like a firefly in the shadows. "We writers are practically gods!"

"Demigods, perhaps." A gaunt figure with a haunted look on his face materialized from the darkness and joined the conversation. "It's we critics who are the *real* gods."

"Ah, Auggie, how are you?" said Max. "I've been looking for you. I wanted you to meet my friend, Frank Matthews." He waved me over before I could slip away. "Frankie, this is the literary critic for the *Times*, August Snipe. Frank's a writer too. Been working on his novel for, what—ten years? But I tell you, once he gets it off the ground, that thing is going to be a masterpiece."

"Everyone, it seems, is a writer these days." Snipe lifted his glass to me as though in salute. He sipped at it thoughtfully. "You know, I once had a friend named Frank Matthews. He was a professional counterfeiter."

"A counterfeiter?" I couldn't tell if he was kidding.

"He was jailed for bank fraud." Snipe chuckled at the memory. "He was a fine fellow."

I didn't know how to take this. "Well," I tried to quip. "Thanks for the career suggestion."

Snipe smiled.

"So how are you enjoying the party?" I said, just to say something.

"Well," shrugged Snipe, "the jazz is derivative, the company largely tedious, and I detest this fusion cuisine. But then"—he smiled a small, tight smile—"I *am* a critic, am I not?" With that he turned and vanished into the crowd.

Magee, by this point, was showing off the flower beds to a group of guests, leading them along the lineup of nodding blooms as though making introductions. "These are night-blooming cereus," she was saying. "I know just how they feel. Even if I was a flower, I'd never be a morning person."

I suddenly needed to use the bathroom. I made my way inside again, only to be swept into a crowd that had gathered around the ethereal woman, who was holding forth in the living room, surrounded by a half-dozen images of herself reflected from the various mirrors. I later discovered she was a famous actress by the name of Guinevere Pilchard.

"I don't know what I can say about working with Bobby Shortman," she declared, "except that it was so . . . spiritual. . . ."

Despite myself, I was drawn into the collective fascination. Her gauzy white clothing trailed about her like filaments of mist, and her eyes, bright and gleaming, were as blue as—no, they *were* the sky.

I really think I'd had too much to drink by this point, but it appeared to me that she was hovering several inches above the floor. She kept saying things like: "Clairvoyance is only déjà vu backwards," and trailing off into silence. But that didn't appear to bother her listeners, mostly men, who seemed about to drop to their knees before the spectacle. I felt a strong urge to attach weights to her feet.

"It's all about sex." I suddenly heard Max's voice, a low, harsh whisper in my ear. "No matter what they think is going on, remove sex from the picture and there'd be nothing happening at all. Have us fixed like dogs and we'd all stay home watching TV. It doesn't matter who's married and who isn't, or if they're actually going to go to bed with any given person—they just want to know they *could* if they wanted to. And who might be available. Mark my words, Frankie, it's sex that drives the whole universe."

He was right. I looked over at the cloud-woman beaming her sunlike smile down upon us; and as I stood there, something came over me. As in a dream, I saw a great fog, like a storm of hormones, wash across the scene. Millions of tiny tadpole-like creatures swarmed through the spermaceous air. I could practically smell the pheromones. *Max is right,* I thought. *It's just a big mating ritual. Our grand ideas, plans, and schemes: it's all about sex.*

I turned to share my insight with Max, but he was on the other side of the room, talking to a woman who was, simply put, one of the largest human beings I'd ever seen. She was decked out with gauzy scarves and a feather boa, and pieces of glittering finery that seemed designed to accentuate rather than disguise her size; and she gestured and spoke with a grace that belied her tremendous bulk. I later found out she was an exotic dancer by the name of Kitten Caboodle who had appeared in Stiffy Phillips's most recent oddball comedy.

As I made my way out I overheard Max saying to her: "Women are very important to me. My mother was a woman, you know."

The bathroom reeked of cigar smoke. I stood there, swaying slightly and staring at myself in the mirrored walls: tux askew, tie unraveling, disheveled hair. Who was this guy, anyway? I didn't recognize him. Someone was already rattling the doorknob.

The next thing I knew, I found myself standing above a fixture that, in my best estimation, I believed to be the toilet. The doorknob rattled again. My head whirled. *What is it about human nature,* I wondered, *that nobody ever believes their first perception that the door is locked?* They always have to try it three or four times before they're convinced. I eyed the toilets; there now appeared to be two of them. They beckoned, and my abdomen gurgled in response. But I resisted. I was pretty sure that, given the choice, I'd have selected the one that wasn't

real—an action that couldn't help but have extremely unpleasant consequences for everyone. I took a deep breath,
turned the knob, and staggered out past the ethereal woman,
who'd been waiting for God knew how long and was standing
out there with her arms crossed, tapping her foot impatiently.

The rest of the evening dissolved into a kind of dream. I remember going out into the driveway, where I started wandering in circles, hoping that might undo the whirling in my
brain. For a time I tried to sort out whether the whirling was
going clockwise or counterclockwise, reasoning that if I circled in the opposite direction that might unwind it more ef-
fectively. But the effort proved too much and I ended up just
having to go on instinct.

I kept stumbling on these scary-looking guys from a band
called Heinous Anus, standing in out-of-the-way places,
smoking joints, or just lurking for the fun of it. They were
pretty fearsome, all right, done up from one end to the other
in the latest scarification designs, with notches taken out of
their ears to boot. I found myself wondering if they were real.

It must've been 2:00 A.M. already. I'd proposed that night,
I think, to three different women. I switched to drinking water. I went up to the kennels for a while and petted the dogs,
who since our walk counted me among their closest friends.

By the time I headed back to the house I was feeling better.
Somebody had lit a bonfire out in the driveway. Ash was

starting to fall from a fire over in the San Infernal Valley. The candles and tiki torches were burning down. There was smoke and ash everywhere. *Everything is burning,* I thought foggily. *Everything is on its way out.*

The party appeared to be winding down. Inside, a handful of diehards had settled into chairs; another group was seated on the floor by the fire; others continued to mill about, drinks in hands. Actually, it was impossible to tell how many people were present, for the mirrored fireplace wall, reflecting back into the other mirrors, seemed to double the size of the room, multiplying its inhabitants several times over.

"She slept with the *plumber*," a woman was saying to Magee in a confidential tone, leaning toward her on the brown felt couch as I entered. "Can you *believe* it?" She was one of those women who always seemed to speak in italics.

An unsettling image of the man's member, several feet long with a suction-cup tip, flashed involuntarily across my mind.

"What are you talking about?" I asked. "A soap opera?"

The woman looked at me. "What are you *on?*" she said. "This is *real*."

Max, on the other side of the room, was carrying on a conversation with Vern Akler—whose body, blocked by a clump of remaining guests, I still couldn't see. But I heard Max's voice boom above the chatter: "Of course we have free will. *I* can do anything I want!"

It was quite a scene, getting all the cars unstacked from behind one another and down the steep, curving driveway.

Max sent me off to direct traffic, and still there was a three-way collision at the midpoint of the slope between two sport coupes and a brand-new Mercury Narcissus. A gaunt form untangled himself from the interior of one of the coupes like an enormous stick figure. It was Snipe.

"Is that any way to drive?!" he shouted in the general direction of the other driver. "Where'd you get your license—the Milwaukee Tractor Club for the Blind?"

"I'm afraid," responded the other, who was in the process of extracting his own rather pear-shaped form from his conveyance, "that this unfortunate incident was caused by nothing more than an unavoidable convergence of conditions: in other words, Fate." This was Vern Akler, of course, who appeared to have successfully retrieved the rest of his body from wherever he'd been keeping it.

The Mercury, oddly enough, turned out to be empty. It had simply slipped its brake and run down the hill of its own accord—and no one, again, had noticed.

"Tell me," I couldn't resist asking Akler as he and I pushed the empty Narcissus off to the shoulder—Snipe had refused, on principle, to participate—"are you *really* a scatologist?"

He looked at me blankly.

At last I made my way back to the house, exhausted, and headed up the stairs. The place was empty except for the interjection guy, who was now asleep on his back on the couch, emitting a string of snores and grunts that didn't sound enormously different from his conversation. Max, still brimming with energy, had taken the dogs out for a run on the beach. I was headed down the hall to the guest-room stairs when I heard a voice from behind Max and Magee's bedroom door, which was slightly ajar.

"Max, is that you?"

I hesitated. "No, Magee. It's me."

"Frank, come in here and help me off with this, would you?"

Heart thudding against my rib cage, I pushed the door open. Inside, I could see a spill of light coming from a dressing room to the left.

"It's this necklace. I can never get the damned thing off."

The room smelled of powder, perfume, smoke. Magee was in a silky dressing gown in front of the mirror. The light from above cast a soft glow upon her features.

"Here, you try." She swiveled on her stool and presented her back to me.

My hands were trembling. A line of fine hair on the nape of her neck disappeared into the open back of her gown. Her vertebrae were strung like pearls beneath her translucent skin. The necklace unfastened easily in my hands.

Magee sighed. "Thanks."

"Are you O.K.?" I asked.

"Oh, I don't know." She let down her hair and shook it out. "Sometimes it all just doesn't seem to add up to very much, you know?"

She lit a cigarette, watched herself shake out the match in the mirror, blew smoke against the glass.

"But, Magee, you have so much. Your home, your marriage. Talent."

She snorted. "What talent?"

"Your writing. I remember it from Boscoe. It's good."

"I don't write anymore, Frank." Her eyes met mine in the mirror. "That's Max's job."

I hesitated. "You have beauty."

"What good is beauty?" Magee looked askance at herself, and I remembered the sleazy producer who'd been trying to pick her up all night. "All beauty does is attract a bunch of creeps."

I didn't answer. I was staring past her at the tangle of jewelry that spilled from her many boxes of earrings, bracelets, and necklaces, open and tumbling across the counter: gold, pearls, unidentifiable stones. Some of it, no doubt, was costume stuff, for Magee was no snob, and valued the funky as much as the sophisticated. But as far as I was concerned, in that rare alchemy Magee possessed, everything she touched turned to gold. Still, something about that heap of sparkling stuff caught my attention. It wasn't that the tangle of hoops and bangles exhibited any recognizable order, although pieces fell together in a certain symmetry. But there were things of beauty here; somehow, in that jumble of bright and glittering things, it seemed there was something fine, and shining, and good.

Back in my room, I'd just begun to peel off my tux when a knock came at the door, causing my normally plodding heart to go into near-fibrillations.

But then Max's voice boomed out: "Frankie, my lad, what do you say we go for a drive?"

"At this hour?" I said through the door. "Max, do you know what time it is?"

"The time, my boy, is always Now!"

I never could say no to Max, and as he seemed resigned to letting me drive, I agreed. I'd had nothing but water to drink for the past three hours, and was feeling reasonably in control of my faculties again. And although I'm a bit loath to admit it—machinery not being a key area of self-definition for me—I couldn't resist having another go at piloting the Ocelot. I slipped my jacket back on and we headed, at Max's suggestion, toward San Melonica, then up Sunrise to where the broad, twisting curves of Mulehauler Drive ascended to the top of the Coast Range. "Go, go, go," Max squealed as I took the turns, pushing the car as hard as I could manage. "More, more, more!" There it was, that strange, high-pitched laugh again, as though something had rattled loose inside him. It was like driving with a three-year-old.

"Hold on." Max grabbed my arm. "Pull over here." We stopped on a hilltop. There was a communications installation with a bunch of satellite dishes behind a barbed-wire-topped fence; scattered around it were a half-dozen picnic tables. It looked to me like a questionable spot to come at night, the kind of place gangs would hang out, or groups of teenage drinkers. There was, in fact, graffiti spattered across many of the boulders. But for now we had it to ourselves. Max mounted a picnic table and stood swaying in his tux, grandly, gloriously drunk. I climbed up beside him. He kept craning his neck as though trying to see something over to the east, I couldn't tell what. "Look!" he pointed. "There it is!" At first I couldn't see what he was pointing at, but then there materialized, as though out of the ether, a string of letters: the hazy outline of the famous Hollywood sign, shining from a distant hillside. "Just think of it," said Max. "That's where Faulkner and Fitzgerald sold their talents to the movie industry and made their fortunes!"

Well, it hadn't happened exactly that way, but I wasn't going to try to argue with Max in his condition. Below us the lights of Los Angeles were spread out across the valley; highways lit with headlights snaked like glowing serpents over the plain. To the north and east I could see the reddish glow of the San Infernal fire. Buildings thrust upward into the brownish, smoldering haze. It looked to me like the gates of Hell.

"Here we are," exulted Max. "The pinnacle. The top. Look! It's ours for the taking. Just like Faulkner and Fitz." His whole body was shaking. He didn't know what to do with himself. "We should create something," he said. "Destroy something. Start a revolution!" Abruptly, he cupped his hands around his mouth and shouted over the drop: "I will have what I will have—and I Will Have It!" I listened as the echoes faded away.

Again he shouted:

"I . . . Am . . . Max Peterson!"

The sound receded, with no response; no one up above seemed inclined to smite Max for his impertinence. Down and away, far into the night, I could hear other noises begin to emerge: sirens, truck engines. A pack of coyotes in the distance were going crazy, yipping and howling like mad things. The moon coasted low above the horizon.

Suddenly Max turned to me and said, "She isn't perfect, you know."

"Who isn't?"

"Magee. She has one eye that's a little smaller than the other—had you noticed? And it's closer to her nose than the other one. And there's a mole on the left side of her neck, which, if you look at it closely, is quite unattractive."

I didn't know how to respond. We both fell silent.

"Max," I said after a long while. "Why did you marry Magee?"

"Because I love her." Max looked at me as though it were the most obvious thing in the world. He turned to gaze over the night. "Frankie, my boy"—he shook his head—"you don't know a thing about love."

And I suppose he was right. I don't know why, but at that moment I took a step back, leaving Max standing between me and the drop.

I slid my hand into my pocket and fingered the slim golden strand I'd left coiled there.

I still had Magee's necklace.

4

In Which I Rediscover Paradise

DON'T MAKE the mistake of thinking that Magee's smoking was glamorous. It was her hacking that woke me the next morning, a prolonged string of coughing sounds, ending with a spell of terrible retching that shook the walls. I emerged from a long, confused dream—someone was auctioning off the moon, I think—and came downstairs to find Magee sitting at the kitchen table in her bathrobe, eating leftovers out of Tupperware with a plastic fork. There was a haze of smoke already in the air and a fresh butt in the ashtray. I swear, I'd never seen anyone smoke like that woman could, and survive. I wondered if she smoked in the shower. I wondered if she smoked during sex.

Actually, Magee had one of the more unusual stories I'd heard of how someone started smoking. It had happened in her freshman year at college; to qualify for a degree in

Boscoe's progressive program, everyone was required to volunteer for a certain number of community service hours. Most of us ended up teaching writing to disadvantaged kids; Magee chose instead to help out with the school's "Kick Your Butts" stop-smoking program. But after seeing people file through by the droves, with only a handful ever able to surrender the habit, she'd decided there must be something to it, and started up herself.

"What are *you* looking at?" Magee asked me in a humorous tone. I must've been studying her a bit closely, trying to see whether what Max had said about her eyes was true.

"Have some breakfast," she said. "We have, let's see, strawberry garbanzo-bean mole sauce . . ."

It amazed me to see her like that, in that old bathrobe at the kitchen table eating leftovers straight out of the Tupperware, as though she were just another human being: an ordinary person.

I'd been trying to learn to meditate at that point for nearly as long as I'd been trying to become the greatest novelist of my generation, and when I went back up to my room after breakfast, that's what I intended to do. But on my way down the hall I noticed the door of Max's study was slightly ajar, and I couldn't resist poking my head inside to have a look. I'd imagined, given the literary figures Max ranked himself among, that I'd find a Dostoyevsky-type garret; but to my surprise, it was a bright, high-ceilinged space with bookshelves lining the walls. An enormous wooden desk sat at the center, with an

old manual typewriter and a pile of scattered papers on it. A
bay window overlooked the garden; beyond was a view along
the Pacific coast that might have stretched all the way to Mexico, if not for the brownish haze that blotted up everything
from Los Angeles southward. I could see a framed cover of
City of Breasts on the wall, its familiar, lurid cityscape of
upward-thrusting buildings and breast-shaped clouds upstag-
ing the more timid, official-looking documents and awards
that surrounded it. A bar in the corner, a leather couch, and a
comfortable-looking green armchair completed the picture.
It seemed an oddly formal arrangement for Max.

I'm sure I would have continued on up to my turret room
at that point, except that there was a piece of paper sticking
up from the typewriter, the same Underwood manual Max
had insisted on using ever since I'd known him—he always
said it made him feel like Hemingway—and I couldn't resist
having a closer look at whatever he was working on.

Stepping over to the desk, I was diverted by a collection
of photographs that stood in a surprisingly tidy lineup on its
surface. A couple of stones and seashells were dotted about,
like a shrine. The largest photo featured a pudgy kid, age
twelve or so, standing on a beach in a pair of polka-dotted
swim trunks: Max, looking a bit bewildered, if the truth be
told. There was something touching about seeing him like
that, little pink belly already spilling over his waistband, before success and cigars and Jack Daniel's got to him, with not
a trace of arrogance upon his features. Behind him stood two
adults who might have been his parents; I didn't remember
him ever saying anything about them, or for that matter, any

relatives coming to visit when we were at Boscoe. Beside this was an older photo, a bit faded, of another couple—grandparents, maybe? The man looked a lot like Max, although a more dignified version thereof; portly rather than paunchy, in a three-piece suit, but sporting the same circular bald spot at the apex of his head.

At the center of the arrangement was a gilt-framed photo of Magee, wearing a wide-brimmed straw hat in a field of daffodils, outshining them all.

What I could write, I thought, if I had an office like this! A view like this.

A wife like this.

I walked to the window and peered over the patio; at the far end I could see the gardener, Jesus, toiling away with one of those bright yellow three-pronged trowels, pulling out spent bulbs. Joss lilies, I think they are called; Magee had pointed them out last night. I felt a little guilty to see him working like that, while all of us were scarcely out of bed.

Max must have taken to writing poetry again—an occupation he'd pursued as far back as our college years, though he'd never received much encouragement for it—for the page in the typewriter went like this:

Our love has vanished like a lost sock.
Remember when we danced
          the delirium shuffle?
The moon hung poised like a lozenge on the enormous tongue
of night.
Streams flowed in the darkness but we could not see them——

Birds called on the other side of the world, but we could not hear.
       I dreamed our names were

                              written

                                     in

                                           air

       but the wind blew them away—
Atlantis sank and rolled away.
In the great dark depths of the sea, fish speak,
       but we cannot understand.

Well, I thought, whoever was out there striving to become the greatest poet of their generation wasn't going to
have to worry about competition from Max Peterson. There
was another page on top of the pile beside the typewriter,
laid out in ordinary paragraphs. I picked it up and looked at
it in the light slanting through the windows:

> *Your eyes are like tiny planets drifting in space. They are like
> boats on the ocean of time and I am the ocean. They are marbles in
> the hands of children, clattering together, being won and lost.
> They are both open and closed, and depthless like water. They are
> soft and yielding like the flesh of clams. They are moist and deli-
> cate, like jewels. They are colored, streaking bullets, tearing open
> the flesh of men's souls. When those eyes meet mine they speak
> more words than a politician on the campaign trail. They are
> pearls built up around the chafe and grit of vision.*

Moist and delicate, like jewels? I thought. Whoever's eyes
they were—Magee's, no doubt, for I couldn't imagine any

other eyes worthy enough to inspire such flights of lyricism—I felt sorry for the treatment they'd received.

Beneath that sheet was another, containing what appeared to be a selection of potential titles:

Soothing the Savage Breast
Goin' Bust
Leave It to Cleavage
Phallus in Wonderland
The Phallus of Damocles
A Town Called Phallus

Jesus, I thought. *Could this guy possibly be for real?* Well, he
appeared to be branching out in new directions, at least,
with the last few titles.

I was starting to feel edgy, jumping at every sound. I'd
gotten drawn in too far, as I always did, and I knew it was
time to get out of there. But as I was turning to leave, I
caught sight of something else. There was a torn bit of paper,
barely visible through the rim of the overflowing glass ashtray beside the typewriter. Through the ashen, smeared
surface I could make out what appeared to be a series of
numbers on it.

I hesitated, turned to go, then turned back again. I lifted
the ashtray. Beneath was a torn-off matchbook cover, on
which a string of smudged digits was written with what
might have been an eyebrow pencil: *116–959–6352.*

Above was a name scrawled in a florid hand: *Kitten
Caboodle.*

Well, it was hard to think about meditating after that, but I gave it a go. I piled up some pillows in the corner of my turret and sat down cross-legged for several minutes, trying to focus on my breath. But the image of those two bodies, clinched in amorous embrace, wouldn't leave my mind.

I supposed that if you were really going to be all-inclusive about the matter, then Kitten Caboodle would have to fit into Max's One Hundred Types: #58, Size XXXXXXXXXXL Exotic Dancer, perhaps. But for some reason I found the thought of the two of them together enormously disturbing. Maybe because it involved a betrayal of Magee; but then, I thought, why should I be bothered by an event that might conceivably leave her free and unencumbered? Images kept filling my head; I kept pushing them away. Then at last it came to me. The problem wasn't so much with Kitten Caboodle, who after all was merely being who she was, and doing a pretty good job of it. It was Max: oversized, slovenly, and falling apart before his time. Maybe picturing Max having sex with *anyone* would have been equally unsettling.

I'd never considered it before.

Finally I was driven to an act of desperation——something only the most dire of circumstances could have provoked me to do: I decided to take a look at my manuscript. I pulled the disheveled mound of paper out of my bag and there, on top, was the opening page, beyond which I hadn't penetrated in weeks——although I must have reread, and rewritten, that passage one hundred and thirty-seven times in the past months:

I recall when I was a child hearing my grandmother talk about what a marvelous thing it was to be a "Finished Man." I sat in an overstuffed armchair in her living room, feet swinging above the floor, while she enumerated the qualities possessed by these highly developed beings: strength, courage, honesty, intelligence. The room, as I remember it now, was dappled in light, sun streaming in through half-opened curtains. I was far from certain, however, that I knew what she was talking about. I'd vaguely heard that there were such things as Finishing Schools for women, and I knew that furniture could be either finished or unfinished. But I'd never heard the term applied to men. Still, as I listened to her speak, an image began to assemble itself in my mind, and I had my first glimmer of understanding about what I might be doing here in the world—something no one had ever been able to adequately explain to me before. I caught a glimpse, that morning, of my destiny: I would, someday, become a Finished Man.

It wasn't until years later that I realized that my grandmother, who was Scandinavian and had been widowed for years, was actually saying how wonderful it would be to meet a "Finnish man." Nevertheless, I carried the notion around with me throughout my childhood and early adolescence—a hazy image of the idealized being I one day hoped to be: the Finished Man.

I thought it wasn't a bad beginning, if a bit overly autobiographical. The problem was, I never could figure out where to go from there. I had visions of my youthful hero facing challenges and overcoming them, engaging in conflicts, conquering crises—but I couldn't imagine what any of these might be. I thought of tracing him through youth and into adulthood, where accidents strange and terrible might befall him, which he might surmount through the power of . . . of . . . Well, at about that point I ran out of thoughts. The rest of the three-hundred-odd pages consisted largely of scraps and beginnings of disconnected scenes, cobbled together by random notes like:

Possible dream that has bearing on his situation?
Sudden deflating of beach ball, symbolic of expectations—
Heart once again broken, he begins anew.

It all added up to what appeared to be a manuscript, but there was no way I could work out how to make the thing hold together. Maybe it was because I couldn't conceive of what it might require, someday, to be Finished.

Who *was* the Finished Man? I had no idea. I'd seemed, in recent months, to have lost track of him entirely.

But all at once, as I leafed through the tattered pages, I was smitten as though by the divine force of inspiration. If Max could write about Magee, why couldn't I? If she could be his muse, why not mine? In fact, I had no doubt that I could do better than he had. I'd have to fictionalize the situation, change the names and so on, like Max had done with *City of Breasts*. But I could worry about that later. I started in:

"L" *words are for Magee: luminous, languorous, lovely; sometimes lurid.*

Well, it was a fresh direction—although something about it seemed a bit familiar, I had to admit. I went on:

Her eyes: was it too much to say they were like suns, or seas? Sometimes green, sometimes shading into yellow, sometimes shifting to gray, set about with specks of light: their color, finally, unnameable . . .

It was better than anything I'd come up with before, at least. Then another approach—an actual situation—occurred to me, for the first time. I wrote:

I'd been in Malomar no more than a few weeks when I felt the madness beginning to come upon me. I hadn't mentioned before, I think, that I suffered from madness: but I tell you now, I have been mad many times.

I am talking about the madness that turns humans into gods, gods into devils, friends into adversaries, creation into rubble, inspiration into nothingness. . . .

I am talking about love.

O.K., it was a bit overwrought, but I could clean that up later too. The important thing was that I seemed to have found my subject at last:

They were a stack of dynamite, Max and Magee, and I was the spark. Slowly, the flame of love—or was it lust, or both?— crept along the fuse, nearer and nearer, until the whole thing was about to go up.

For years, I'd dreamed of becoming Magee's lover. But before long, I would find myself struggling against that possibility with all my might.

People often ask me: "Why do you write?"

Call it a sort of release.

I was deep into the work when a knock came and my door creaked open. I leapt to my feet with a guilty start, pen clutched in my hand. It was Magee.

"Throes of inspiration?" she lilted.

"Throes of *some* sort," I answered.

If only she knew.

I slid a blank sheet of paper over the one on which I'd been working.

"Hey," Magee said, "Max is still sleeping. What do you say we take the dogs for a walk on the beach?"

It was a fine afternoon, only a moderate haze over the water, a breeze from the north pushing the smog southward. The tide was low and the wet flats stretched out forever, shimmering in the sun. It was literally the perfect day, and being out there with Magee was like walking in wonderland, the Land of Oz.

"They say Bobby Zipperman lives somewhere down in the Enclave. I've never seen him, though. Apparently he's a bit of a recluse." Magee pointed along the beach to where the community began: Celebrity Central, step out onto the sand from your living room. It is a tricky thing to stay private on the California seafront, especially in an area as populous as this, for the area below the high-water mark is considered public property; anyone is allowed access, anytime, as long as they remain below the tide line. But the Enclave was well situated, with a creek cutting off access from the south and steep cliffs with headlands that blocked access from the north. We'd had to slip through a torn fence at a building site to reach it ourselves, for there was no formal passage to the beach, even for neighborhood residents.

Still, there was a handful of celebrity-seekers wandering about who'd figured out how to get in one way or another: I could identify them by the binoculars permanently fastened to their eyes. Alpha—or was it Omega? Even Magee couldn't tell them apart—had developed a pastime involving these intruders that seemed to amuse him no end, which I witnessed for the first time that day. He spotted one of them from afar, a woman in purple slacks, studying a beachfront home through her lenses. His head cocked to one side as though he were taking aim; I could see the muscles tighten beneath his brindled hide.

"No, Alpha . . . or Omega," Magee said in a warning tone. "Alpha, no. Omega? . . . No!" All at once he set off down the beach at a dead run, with astounding speed for his tremendous bulk, legs and tail flying, sand going everywhere, gaining momentum as he went, till he was barreling along like an enormous cannonball, straight toward the unsuspecting celebrity-seeker. When he ran full tilt like this he looked absolutely mad, for his eyes rolled back in his head, and his tongue lolled from between his jowls, streaming with slobber.

The victim must have heard the thud of approaching paws, loud as hoofbeats, and dropped the binoculars just in time to see an enormous, slavering beast, jaws agape, bearing down on her like some terrifying creature from a nightmare. She froze in position, then turned to run; but at the last moment the mastiff veered to the side, spewing sand and leaving her unharmed. I couldn't be quite sure of the creature's intent—whether it was to terrify, or just a misguided effort to entice the stranger into a game of tag. In any case, the Enclave should have hired us to work security, for I doubt if any of these intruders, having survived the experience once, would ever be back.

I watched Magee, barefoot and blue-jeaned (she refused to wear shorts, on principle, as being too Californian), stalking across the mudflats, cuffs rolled up above her ankles. Dark wisps of hair trailed from beneath her broad-brimmed sun hat as she poked here and there amidst the tide pools. If I forgot who I was, I could almost imagine my dreams fulfilled: she and I walking out here together with our dogs on another flawless day.

As much as I could find to dislike about LA, coming as I did from the East Coast, there was still California, upon whose ideal form the blight of Los Angeles was overlaid like a cancer. And that form *was* ideal. The Pacific! There was no sea like it; those huge swells humping up in crisp cylinders from beneath that oh-so-perfect surface, rolling in with metronomic precision, like sound waves emanating from some distant bell. That blue! So crisp and clean and translucent and just . . . damned . . . blue that I could hardly bear to look upon it. And the sunset glow upon the water every evening, red and yellow, orange and purple, like being in a dream; the way the waves left their imprints on the damp canvas of sand, picking up the brightness of sky, changing into shapes of things that never were, then evaporating like memories before your eyes. And even the gray days, when the fog never lifted, and you walked amidst the dankness and the ghostly chill, shapes of mist swirling about like forgotten ancestors—the Chumash, who lived here before, and their rainbow bridge to eternity.

Then above us was the Coast Range, hot and dry, dotted with agave and manzanita; and if you climbed high enough, as I sometimes did in the hills above my aunt's house, you might see the fog pour through a cleft in the mountains like the water it was, a river in the sky. And the enormous, spreading oaks on the hillsides, and the tawny fields of wild oats, sown far and wide, growing wherever they pleased; and in the spring, the orange sprawl of California poppy and the purple lupine, the pink of owl clover and red Indian paintbrush, and the enormous phallus-like stalks of the agave, thrusting skyward in a single flowering erection before meeting their end.

Everything wild and natural about Southern California was infinitely pleasing to me, while everything human seemed small and petty and shallow. Compared to the liberation and dream of California, my East Coast upbringing had been a narrow, claustrophobic nightmare. Los Angeles might be the very pit of Hell, but California—California was paradise. Malomar was where the two worlds collided.

The cloud-woman at the party had been right. California was the golden land: Shangri-La, El Dorado, Eden made flesh. And Magee was its goddess. California, at its best, just seemed impossible, the promised land, too good to be true.

And in the end, I suppose, it was.

We stood there for a long time, Magee and I, watching the pelicans glide above the waves, so low it seemed the next one must engulf them. But it never did, for they'd ride the air currents over the rim to drop into the next trough—so close to the surface and it seemed they never had to flap. And every so often there'd be the sudden turn and *sploosh!* of one diving for a mackerel, and it'd come up floating and gulping on the water, enormous gullet upturned, transformed in a moment from grace itself to the droll cartoon figures they became whenever they weren't airborne.

We poked among the tide pools, which for some reason I found very moving. Maybe because the universes they contained were so small, because these worlds were destroyed every few hours, whenever the tide came back in.

"An apocalypse every six hours," said Magee. "Imagine that!"

Here were huge orange and purple starfish I picked up to show Magee, twice the size of my hand, hundreds of suction-cup holdfasts squirming about the undersides of their arms. She surprised me by wanting to run her fingers across their bumpy surfaces, by picking up bits of kelp and dead things— even letting mud snails crawl across her palm. This woman, I thought, was afraid of nothing. Her green eyes danced like light on water, or by turns became studious and serious; and sometimes she'd take my hand to climb across a boulder, or

jump from one rock to another, to show me some new discovery. There were sea urchins, black and spiny to poke yourself on, and abalone, coasting their way across the rock so
slowly you could scarcely see them move; mussels, and
limpets, and tiny fishes that darted this way and that, gleaming
in the sun. The sea anemones were Magee's favorites: delicate,
half-transparent, filled with light. If you looked into the tide
pools at just the right angle you could see the reflection of
your face, backed by their arms that seemed to wave about
from behind your eyes, like the very tentacles of thought.

I found an abalone shell, flawless and unbroken, its
mother-of-pearl interior gleaming with all the colors of the
spectrum, and gave it to Magee as a tribute, a kind of offering.

"It's lovely," she said. "I can use it as an ashtray."

We walked far to the north that afternoon, where the cliffs
loomed close above the beachfront. Headlands jutted into
the water, and would have cut off our travel but for the
miraculously low tide that seemed to part the sea before us;
and everything I saw was holy, holy, holy.

"Someone once told me"—Magee squinted at the cliffs
that tilted above us as we walked—"that there's a place up
there, somewhere along this stretch of coast—a hidden alcove, like a hermitage built into the cliff wall, that you can't
see from below unless you look up at exactly the right time
of day and happen to catch a glint of sunlight off one of the
window panels. My friend Sarah saw it once just as the sun

was setting—a gleam of light from above that caught her curiosity."

That look of absorption came over Magee's face that she always got when she was telling a story, and I remembered the long talks we'd had sometimes back at Boscoe, sitting out on the common at 3:00 A.M., discussing everything from astronomy to zoology, and telling stories from our childhoods.

"Sarah said there was nobody around; she had the beach all to herself. She managed to find a way up the slope, gravel sliding beneath her feet, until she came out onto a stone ledge that blocked the view from below. To her amazement, she found a windowed front wall, set back into a recess in the cliff. She pushed on the door; it creaked open and she stepped inside. There she found a single room, with a bare wooden bunk and a table made of driftwood and a handmade chair by the window that looked out onto the ocean, maybe seventy-five feet below.

"There was a shelf set into the wall, with all these fantastic old books on it: Milton, Plato, a complete edition of Shakespeare. She found a tattered copy of *Madame Bovary* and an early edition of *Anna Karenina,* a couple of novels by Nathanael West, Faulkner's *The Sound and the Fury.* Sarah said it looked like the place hadn't been disturbed for years; none of the books dated past the forties. Who knows how long whoever built it might have lived there, secretly, cut off from the modern world, the Great Depression and the World Wars, the atom bomb. Isn't that a wonderful idea, Frank?" She looked at me, eyes shining. "No one would know where to find you. Just spend your days reading those great classics, looking over the ocean, with the birds and the fish and the whales . . ."

"That's quite a story." I could see it in my mind's eye as clearly as if I'd been there myself. "What happened?"

"It was getting dark and Sarah had to find her way down the cliff while she could still see. She tried to mark the place with piles of rock, but the tide came in and took them away. She told me she searched and searched but never could find it again. It was as though it had never existed."

I thought about the secret alcove and its unknown builder a lot after that. He—for I assumed it was a he, some lost soul from the Depression years, who'd stumbled on his place in paradise—must have hauled the materials up there piece by piece, secretly, probably at night. Even back then it couldn't have been legal, not in America, to build your own place back in the cliff and live there, without paying rent or taxes to anyone. I imagined him working out there by moonlight, the crash of the sea covering the sound of his hammering, the moon like a single great eye watching him, working for a few days or a week every month until it was finished, and he could live his life out there.

I was to spend many days in the months to come looking for the secret alcove. Maybe I was never searching in the right place at the right time. Maybe the sun never hit at the right angle at exactly the right moment. I even looked by moonlight. There were miles of coastline, after all; I guess I shouldn't have been surprised that it was so hard to find. But somehow, I knew Magee's friend hadn't been lying. Somehow, I knew it must be there.

Who had lived there? I continued to wonder. Perhaps it was the Finished Man.

What an afternoon I had, out there on the beach with Magee! For a few hours there was no suffering in the world, no warfare; no wildfires in the hills, no impending earthquakes, no Saint Achille's fault—no faults of any kind. No sorrow; no heartbreak, no hurricanes in Siam, no warfare in Ceylon; no governments, sickness, old age, or death. No unfinished novels. There was only perfection, whole and entire. Magee and I. For the first time in my life, I'd experienced what the poets and sages had all been talking about: a moment of grace.

Stop, time! I thought. *Whoever's in charge, stop it right here. This is what you were after when you started the whole thing up in the first place. If you move on from here you'll only screw it up.*

But whoever they are, they weren't listening, as usual, and they did move on. *That's the problem with God,* I thought, *whoever he, she, or it is. He doesn't know when to leave well enough alone.*

He's never Finished.

Like all dreams, our perfect afternoon at last came to an end, and we went back home; and Max, great lumpy Max, was awake, and grumpy, until he had a drink under his belt—and then he drove me back out through the cleft in the Coast Range that was Malomar Canyon to my aunt's house, and all I could think about was the hidden alcove, and my golden, glorious afternoon with Magee.

Before I left the castle, I'd slipped into Magee's dressing room and put her gold necklace back in its box where it belonged. But I couldn't resist taking something in its place: an earring, a simple silver hoop, just for a while, on loan.

There's an old European custom my grandmother told me about, that whenever you see a new moon you're supposed to reach into your pocket and turn over whatever silver you find there—whether for simple good luck, or in hopes that it would multiply, I was never sure. Now as we drove, sweeping in turns and broad curves between the browning hills, and I looked out the window and listened to Max, I reached into my pocket and turned that silver hoop over again, and again, and again.

5

In Which I Start Writing Again and Go on My First Date in Three Years

 *"TALK TO me about money," she whispered.*

"What?"

"Money." She ran her hand up my thigh.

"Thousands," I began awkwardly. "Millions. Dollar signs."

"That's it."

"Bank accounts. Federal reserve notes. Blue-chip stocks."

"Yes," she coaxed. "Yes."

"Investments. Interest. Speculation. Windfalls."

She was growing more and more excited. Her eyes shone like diamonds.

"Gems," I went on. "Gold bullion. Servants. Yachts. Country estates."

"Yes, yes!" She threw herself on me, practically tackled me.

"Fine china," I muttered between sloppy kisses. "Country

clubs!" She grabbed at my chest, bit at my neck. "Manicured lawns! Croquet!"

And we sank together, helpless, into a bottomless sea of passion.

This wasn't an excerpt from Max's next novel, as one might think—although I was beginning to see how he developed his style. Spend any time in Los Angeles, and it just grew in you. Actually, this was a scene I felt compelled to write for *my* novel, after my date with Molly, from Pacific Palaces. Or was it Polly, from Redundant Beach? Magee, you see, had gotten into her head the misguided notion—for a time it was practically a mission—that she needed to fix me up with one of her friends. Maybe Max had talked to her about my dismal sexual history, I don't know, but lately, every other time I saw them, Magee had a different acquaintance she wanted me to meet.

A couple of months had gone by since the afternoon I'd met Max on the pier. I'd settled into a routine: hang out with Max and Magee two or three nights a week, then, every couple of weekends, a party.

"Friday the twenty-seventh!" Max would announce. "Friday the tenth! Why be bound by a silly number like thirteen?"

The summer grew drier and drier; a permanent haze of smoke hung over the city from fires burning in Angora, Sleepy Valley, St. Bernard. When the wind blew the right way, it rained ash.

Meanwhile, my inability to either stay away from Malomar or to find a graceful way to evade Magee's matchmaking resulted in a series of the most peculiar encounters I'd ever had the misfortune to engage in. Consider Alice, from Rue de Fleurs Canyon:

> *"I like scars," she said, her forefinger stroking its way along my wrist. "I once had a boyfriend, he was put back together after a car wreck. They had to strip all his skin off and put it on again. His whole body was a network of scars. His skin looked like a map, one territory against the next, and all the borderlines between. You could see every place he'd suffered. It was right there in front of your eyes." She looked me over appraisingly. "Got any you'd like to show me?"*

The encounter described at the beginning of the chapter—the one with the money fetishist—was, I admit, slightly fictionalized. We didn't sink into any bottomless sea of passion. Instead, I excused myself to go the bathroom, and fled.

Come to think of it, that's what I did with Alice, the scar queen, too.

But the good news was, I'd started writing again. With all the new material coming my way, how could I do otherwise? Being around Max and Magee was inspiring enough, even without the extraneous adventures. Maybe it was that I wanted to outdo him. Maybe it was that I wanted to live up to her.

In any case, I got onto a new work schedule as the summer grew hotter and more and more smoke swept down from the surrounding hills. I'd get up at 11:00 or so and have breakfast. Then I'd close the windows to keep out the smoke, and spend the rest of the day sweating, coughing, and writing. My aunt Clara, you see, didn't believe in air-conditioning. She always insisted that the heat out West was "dry heat." According to her, you didn't feel it the same way you did back in New Jersey. And she was right. In the East the humidity seemed to force its way into your body till you had sweat dripping out of every pore; in the West every molecule of moisture was sucked *out* of your body, till you felt as desiccated as old King Tut. We were coming up to the last of my agreed-upon months at her house, although neither of us, as yet, had mentioned it. She occasionally asked me, in a fashion sometimes timid and sometimes resigned, how the work was going.

I gave the same answer I'd given everyone who asked that question for the last ten years: "Fine, fine."

I tried not to think about it much, but I felt like Dorothy in *The Wizard of Oz,* in that scene with the giant hourglass. I had no idea what I was going to do when my time ran out.

I'd been driving the Trojan Hearse, which had fallen on considerably less bountiful times than its halcyon days as Max's tryst-mobile. You need a certain brand of panache to roll up in a funeral limo without putting off your prospective partner, and I guess I didn't have that touch. But Max had loaned the old behemoth to me on a semipermanent basis, so at least I had the freedom to come and go as I pleased. And I had to admit I liked the way it looked, whizzing down the freeway alongside all the Mazdas and Volvos and BMWs.

Trillion Oaks was so far from anywhere you'd actually

want to spend time that there was no alternative but to drive. To an Easterner like myself, this seemed an odd way to live. But that's what life is like in Los Angeles. Any event is bracketed by a round-trip automobile ride of at least an hour, and all it takes to extend that period indefinitely is to get caught in one of the horrendous traffic jams that can rise, like the jaws of a steel trap, to engulf you at any moment. As Magee put it: "In Southern California you're always very close to eternity—because that's how long you spend in traffic every day." In fact, my entire memory of those months at my aunt's house is one long, confused nightmare of inter-locking, smog-ridden highways. I got to know them all: the San Diablo Freeway, the Vultura, the Hellbourne, the San Maniacal. . . .

I often wondered how the commuters stood it, sacrific-ing enormous segments of their lives daily to the god—or demon—of transport. But then, maybe people liked it that way. The freeway became a home away from home for them. They had their CD players, their air conditioners, their books on tape; the limousines even had bars and television sets. Some of the big limos were so enormous I pictured hot tubs, dining rooms, cabaret acts.

Marjorie, from Venus Beach, told me she once heard of a couple who carried on an affair by meeting every morning in the same traffic jam and trysting amidst the stalled automo-biles, stopping between thrusts to put the car into drive and inch forward a foot or two before resuming their embraces. Then she suggested we try it ourselves.

I excused myself to use the bathroom.

The other thing about Los Angeles is that just about everyone, no matter their profession, regards themselves as an artist of one stripe or another: writer, actor, filmmaker, musician. Which the following encounter, which took place when we were tooling around town in the Ocelot one afternoon, and Max insisted on driving all the way out to Belle Heir because it was one of the few places you could still find a full-service gas station.

It was the kind of hellishly smoggy day that is the norm in the Los Angeles summer. The air was green; the air was purple; the air was colors it had no right to be. We set out onto the San Diablo Freeway, jetting along in the Occie, as Max called it, sometimes cutting out of the traffic altogether when it got too thick and shooting along the shoulder for miles at a stretch.

"Look at all the houses," mused Max. "Row upon row of them. Imagine the countless lives flashing by! And they all eat and drink and love, just like we do, and they all think their lives are every bit as important as the next guy's." He sighed. "You know, Frankie, it seems to me that some people exist just so others like you and me can do what we want to do. I imagine a whole nation of citizens out there, struggling and striving and sweating, so we don't have to."

It was quite a vision he had, old Max, I had to admit.

At last we pulled into the Toxoco station in Belle Heir.

"Fillerup, West," said Max to the attendant, a skinny, sunburnt fellow with an eager look about him. "How's the screenplay going?"

"It's going," said the attendant. "It's bustin' along like no-body's business."

"What's it been now, five years?"

The attendant took a minute to do some arithmetic on his fingers. "Going on six. But after the rewrites are done, mark my words: the world's gonna hear from me!" He shoved the pump nozzle into place, then came around and stood by the passenger window, looking at me as though he wanted something. I rolled it down.

"They call me West," he said, extending a hand. "West Covina. You a writer too?"

"Yes, I am." His grip proved to be more suited to gas noz-zles than human flesh. "I'm Frank. Frank Matthews."

"That a pen name?"

"Well, it's the one on my birth certificate. I guess they must've written that with a pen." It wasn't the best joke, I admit, but the possibility that jokes existed at all seemed to go right past the guy.

"I'm telling you," he said, "you gotta have a pen name if you're gonna succeed in this business. When I pulled in from Little Rock I knew right away I was going to have to come up with something catchy. So I took the name of the first town I stopped in. Did a baptism ceremony for myself in my motel room with a can of Coors."

Could this guy possibly be for real? I found myself look-ing around for hidden cameras.

"My real name was Glen Dale," he told me. "But let me tell you, I'm in the thick of it here. It's been nothing but writers pulling in all afternoon. It's the Day of the Writer around here." I'd heard the pump click off a while back, but there was no shutoff switch on West Covina. Max had tuned out of the conversation entirely and, despite the giant DANGER: NO SMOKING signs, was lighting a fresh cigar.

The attendant still stood there looking at me.

"What's the subject of your screenplay?" I asked.

"It's a sex comedy. I'm calling it *Service with a Smile.*"

Max was starting to rev the engine, and the guy seemed to catch on that this was a cue to pull out his nozzle and put the gas cap back on. But quicker than Max could say, "Put it on my tab," West was leaning in again through my window.

"Know any producers?" he was saying, as Max put the Ocelot in gear and pulled slowly away, trying to disengage the guy's elbows from where they'd lodged on the door panel. "I've already got an idea for the sequel. I'm gonna call it *Fillerup, West.*"

"Catchy," I said as we pulled off. "See you again sometime, huh?"

"Never fear," he shouted after us. "You haven't seen the last of West Covina!"

"Those are words that would fill a *lot* of people with fear," said Max as we revved off in the getaway car.

The first brush I had with actual consummation in my series of amorous adventures was with Valerie from Culvert City (which Max insisted on calling "Vulva City," causing even the almost-impossible-to-embarrass Magee to turn red and chide him). Valerie wasn't as intimidating as the others, perhaps because she came from more humble beginnings. We ended up getting horizontal, all right, but just at the point it seemed like it might go somewhere, she came out with:

"Just think of it! While we're lying here in bed, there are people out there being shot and dying and starving. There's famine and war. People coming down with incurable diseases. Plagues, torture, and pestilence. Bombs dropping."

The notion caused my strategic defense system, which had been standing at readiness, to lose a certain degree of its firing power. But her eyes were gleaming. The idea didn't seem to diminish her sex drive in the slightest. If anything, it seemed poised to rouse her to a frenzy.

I had to excuse myself to go to the bathroom.

Things went downhill from there. There was Jane from Tarzona, and Patricia from Morona Del Rey. And here are a few that may or may not be fictionalized:

Eloise, whose idea of foreplay was to lie on her back with arms outspread in the pose of Christ, crying, "Impale me!"

Pamela, who'd lost her virginity in the local cemetery and ever since couldn't get aroused without talk of coffins and gravestones.

Barbara, who was convinced she was dead already.

Roxanne, whose obsession with "outie" navels led her to reject me before we cleared the bedroom door.

Regina, who turned out to not be Regina at all but Reggie—a fact I didn't discover until I'd begun removing her dress.

Although I did, remarkably, succeed eventually in

consummating several of these encounters, none of them amounted to anything in the end. The only way I could even get aroused, to tell you the truth, was to think about Magee.

This was a strategy I'd already been using for years.

The real question was: why did I keep going back for more? After all, nobody was dragging me out to Malomar to see them. Well, Max did just about drag me, several times. But I might have resisted.

The obvious answer was that I couldn't stay away from Magee. I knew it was an impossible infatuation and that my whole obsession with her was misguided, to say the least. But that didn't mean I could do anything about it. Love is an addiction, make no mistake; and once it has its hooks in you, the habit is impossible to break.

But then, I couldn't stay away from Max either. He was, after all, my supplier.

If the truth be known, I think I was becoming a little obsessed with both of them.

6

In Which My Parents Come for a Visit and Magee Smokes a Cigar

BY THE time fall rolled around, Magee seemed to have gotten over her matchmaking mania. Perhaps it was that she'd given up on me, or maybe she'd just run out of friends. Her impulse toward community, however, found a new direction when she heard my mother and my uncle Charlie were coming west for a visit. She insisted on inviting us all, along with my aunt Clara, out to Malomar for dinner.

"Aw, Magee," Max had protested. "No offense, Frankie, but people's mothers . . . well, I just never know how to behave around them, if you know what I mean."

"You never know how to behave around anyone, Max," said Magee. "And besides, it's nearly Thanksgiving."

By my count Thanksgiving was still four weeks away. But I could never refuse Magee anything, and neither, apparently, could Max, for the following week I found myself, along with my aunt Clara, my mother, and my uncle Charlie, traveling out to Malomar to meet them, several hours before sunset.

Uncle Charlie was my stepfather, although I never referred to him that way. My parents had been separated since I was a young child. The official story was that my father, who had been an industrial engineer, had first abandoned the family, then developed a progressive neurological disease, and finally went a bit off the deep end and had to be confined to a home. He was replaced almost immediately, as it seems to me now, by his younger brother, my uncle Charlie, who shared many of his qualities.

I went to see my father occasionally, from my teenage years on, although this was not particularly encouraged by the family. He was housed in a dreadful-looking institution outside New Brunswick. My father did not seem to regard insanity as a particular barrier to his career, and he spent his time in the institution coming up with designs for useful items that might help the world. On one of my visits he told me about his latest invention: non-sticking tape.

"For things," he explained, "that don't need to be stuck to anything. And it's easy to get off the roll!"

He considered himself to be an "industrial theorist" as well, and could hold forth on the subject with far greater endurance than sane people like myself could muster. "The only way to improve on planned obsolescence," he once told me, "is to create products that are out of date *before* they're produced."

Seemed to me he should've been released immediately

and appointed to the President's Commission on Trade and Development.

The strange thing was, my father and my uncle Charlie looked so similar that they might almost have been twins. I don't want to dig too deeply into the psychology behind this, but there ought to be a name for whatever complex my mother and Uncle Charlie were exhibiting in marrying each other so soon after my father's departure. Old Freud would certainly have had a field day with it.

Although I was only five or six at the time my father left, I had never taken to calling my uncle Charlie "Dad," or referring to him as my stepfather, or anything other than Uncle Charlie.

Even my mother called him Uncle Charlie.

Max sent a cab to pick us all up at my aunt Clara's house in Trillion Oaks on the appointed afternoon, since my mother refused on principle to travel in the hearse. "I'm planning on waiting a few more years," she said, "for *that* particular experience."

The cabbie greeted me, "Every time they send me out here there's more of you. What, are you all breeding or something?"

The drive out to Malomar was an exercise in claustrophobia. Aunt Clara sat in the front seat. I ended up sandwiched in the back between my mother and Uncle Charlie, neither of whom had been farther west than Pittsburgh, so they'd have a chance to look out the windows.

They didn't seem overly impressed.

"I thought California was supposed to be the Golden State," my mother sniffed, gazing over the parched hills. "This is just plain *brown*."

"It's the West, Mom," I tried to explain. "When it's not the rainy season, it's the dry season. That's why we have so many fires."

My mother was like someone from another time, perhaps the forties or fifties. I'm not quite sure how this happened. Maybe it arose naturally from living in Newark; but every era from the sixties onward seemed to have escaped her notice entirely. If you mentioned the Beatles her eyebrows would raise with a quizzical expression, as though she'd once known what you were talking about but had forgotten. And if, God forbid, the name Martin Luther King came up, she was likely to say, "Oh, wasn't he that nice Negro man from somewhere down South?" The women's movement had passed her by completely.

She wore her hair in a kind of bouffant—at least, that's what I think it's called; the actual name may be lost in the mists of history—with a big, poofy platinum top and the ends turned up at the tips. It took an entire afternoon at the hairdresser each week to create the effect. Mom was God's greatest gift to the American hairspray industry.

"Where are the oaks?" burst out Uncle Charlie. That was his way. He'd go along forever without saying a thing, letting my mother run on and on, but all the time there'd be something ruminating inside him, and suddenly it would erupt, regardless of whatever was happening at the time.

"The oaks?" I said.

"They call it Trillion Oaks, don't they?"

He was right, you know. Near as I could tell, there were only a couple dozen oaks left in Trillion Oaks. The rest had been cut down to make way for shopping malls and housing developments.

My mother cut in: "I don't understand why they don't just *water* them."

"The oaks?"

"Those awful dry hills. We'd never let our lawns look like that back East."

"Mom, I don't think you get it. Once you're up in the hills, it's basically wilderness. We're talking miles and miles of open land. Besides, we're having a drought."

"Hmmph," replied my mother, clutching her handbag closer to her abdomen, as she always did when she felt threatened by something—whether to protect the handbag or herself, I was never sure.

"I wouldn't want to have to *mow* those hills now, I'll tell you that," said Uncle Charlie, with a sparkle in his eye that showed he was ribbing her.

"Oh, do shut up, Uncle Charlie," snapped my mother.

They were quite a pair. Her nerves were as delicate as a china cabinet in an earthquake zone. And their relationship was riddled with faults.

No sooner had I stepped free of the cab than Alpha and Omega, who Max had forgotten to confine to their kennels, came bounding up to greet me. Alpha—or perhaps it was Omega—

leaped up and plunked his paws against my chest with such enthusiasm that he pinned me against the hood. While he pro-
ceded to drown me in slobbering dog-kisses, his partner
commenced such a round of barking and snarling at the new-
comers that my aunt Clara, who was "constitutionally timid," as
she herself put it, started to cry. My mother, meanwhile, was
doing her best to clamber atop the roof of the cab, and making
a pretty good effort at it, despite her high-heeled shoes.

My uncle Charlie's only response to the situation, however, was to cry out: "A dog! A panic in a pagoda!"

This might seem an odd response to the uninitiated. But
my uncle Charlie was not your average fellow. He was prone
to intellectual obsessions, which he tried on, then took off
again, like clothing. His most recent one was word games,
which I'd unfortunately triggered by getting him a book on
anagrams last Christmas by the writer Myra Phunes. The
current manifestation of his condition was palindromes:
those rare examples of verbal symmetry that spell the same
backward as they do forward. "Race car," he'd say, with a significant look, and wink slyly. Then: "Madam, I'm Adam" or
"Rats live on no evil star." Combined with his near-perfect
gift of recall, this obsession was a terrifying thing. He'd been
waiting all afternoon for a chance to use one of the numerous examples he'd already committed to memory. Now that
he was started there'd be no switching him off.

"Go, dog!" he was shouting. "Goddamn! Mad dog!"

Max, meanwhile, was trying to call off the canines and tip
the cab driver at the same time, while I, with a hundred-
pound mastiff on my chest, was in no position to do much

except try to get a breath in between slaps of that huge wet tongue, which was larger than many a towel I've seen. I wasn't at all certain whether my new status as friend was in any way preferable to being the beasts' enemy.

"Go deliver a dare, vile dog!" shouted Uncle Charlie. "Dog, no poop on God!"

These obsessions generally lasted a year or two; there was nothing to do but wait them out.

At last Jesus the gardener appeared, as though by divine intervention, and hauled the dogs off to their kennels. Max insisted on embracing and kissing each one of us on the cheek—even my uncle Charlie, who turned slightly pink, responding: " 'Tis Ivan on a visit!"

"Palindromes!" Max said. "I used to play with those as a kid." He grinned and his eyes lit up. "Nurse, I spy gypsies: run!"

You had to love the guy, in a certain way. He was like a great, sloppy puppy himself.

"Oy, oy, a tonsil is not a yo-yo," answered my uncle Charlie.

As we walked into the house, Max was clapping Uncle Charlie on the back and asking: "Do geese see God?"

To which Charlie, clearly delighted, answered: "Evil I did dwell, lewd did I live!"

We stepped into the front room and I introduced them all around. Magee's hair, which had transformed entirely since the last time I saw her, was blond and freshly cut into a page-boy. She had a sort of flapper outfit on, with a dress that clung to her like Saran Wrap. I couldn't take my eyes off her.

"I'm so sorry about the dogs." Magee put her arm around Aunt Clara and handed her a tissue. "Max just can't seem to keep them under control. They're really quite harmless, once you get to know them."

"I'm not quite sure"—Clara blew her nose loudly, and sniffled a bit—"that I want to get to know them anytime soon." She examined her curly gray hair in one of the mirrored walls and adjusted the polka-dot scarf she always wore on special occasions.

"All I ever wanted was a whippet," said Magee. "Just one. But Max insisted . . ."

My aunt, who was a bit of a recluse and had probably experienced little physical contact for decades, appeared to be blossoming under her hostess's attentions. Perhaps, I thought, Magee's outfit reminded her of her girlhood. "A whippet?" Clara repeated. "Isn't that a sort of greyhound? My father used to bet on the dogs. . . ."

Magee embraced my mother next. "You have a wonderful son," she said. At this Mom and I both beamed. "And you must be Uncle Charlie. I've heard so much about you."

To which Charlie, whose rounded, moustachioed figure, replicating itself in the many mirrors, made us appear to be surrounded by a legion of organ-grinders, replied: "Elf farm raffle."

My mother groaned.

While Magee showed my mother and aunt around the castle ("How nice," my mother exclaimed, primping herself enthusiastically. "Mirrors everywhere!"), Max and I took Uncle Charlie down to the ballroom for a game of hoops. Incredibly, he was even better than Max. He trounced me solidly in our first game of one-on-one, then took on Max and beat him eleven to ten, winning with an incredible long shot that skimmed between the chandeliers, hit once against the backboard, and dropped into the hoop with scarcely a whisper. Max was so amazed, his jaw dropped open and his cigar fell to the floor.

"Cigar?" said Uncle Charlie. "Toss it in a can. It is so tragic!"

"Boy, they really teach you to play basketball out in Newark, don't they?" said Max.

If so, I thought, it hadn't worked on me.

Afterward, Uncle Charlie snuck one of Max's cigars, saying to me: "Your mom won't let me smoke anymore."

No, it wasn't a palindrome. He was just talking.

We came back to find Magee and my mother and Aunt Clara standing in the garden. "Horses . . ." Magee was saying. "They were the most remarkable things—"

"Aw, Magee," said Max, "you're not going to bore everyone with your horse dream again, are you?"

With that he proceeded to hold forth in detail on every modification he'd ever performed on the castle, which had first been built by a visionary Peruvian perfume importer in the 1960's but had fallen into disrepair, until Max realized the vast potential inherent in the structure and . . . and . . .

We gathered on the patio to watch the sunset. The wildfires had simmered down for the season, and if you ignored the brownish smear of smog along the horizon, the evening was idyllic.

"Max," Magee said, "aren't you going to offer our guests anything to drink?" She'd sent Lupe and Esperanza home once they'd finished preparing the dinner; it embarrassed her to be waited on except when staging a major event.

"Yes, Your Majesty," Max responded with a mock bow. He'd been looking out to sea, perhaps pondering more palindromes to hurl at my uncle. "Drinks, anyone?"

"Murder for a jar of red rum," said my uncle.

"Not sure we've got any of that, Uncle Charlie," put in Magee. She'd already taken to calling him Uncle Charlie too. It was practically an involuntary response. "But you might ask Max. *He's* the expert here on just about everything."

What was up with the two of them tonight? I wondered.

Uncle Charlie shrugged: "Lager, sir, is regal."

"Uncle Charlie," laughed Magee, "how do you do it? You're so clever!"

Encouragement, of course, was the worst possible response to a condition like Uncle Charlie's.

"Claret, please, for myself and Clara," said my mother.

"I'm with Uncle Charlie," I said.

"Our home in New England . . ." my mother was saying to Magee, touching up her makeup in the mirror of her compact, when Max returned with the drinks. He'd been gone for quite a while, no doubt composing the toast he proceeded to offer in Uncle Charlie's honor: "Campus motto: Bottoms up, mac!"

Although everyone in my family had grown up in

Newark, my mother had somehow succeeded in convincing herself and my uncle Charlie that we qualified as New Englanders. "Our ancestors came over on the boat just after the *Mayflower*," she'd just finished explaining. "The next one. The . . ." She always got fuzzy on this point.

"The *Juneflower*?" I'd put in.

Whatever the vessel was, she appeared to be under the impression it had landed in Atlantic City.

"Mom," I protested now, for the umpteenth time in my existence. "New Jersey is *not* generally considered to be part of New England."

She turned upon me with that long-suffering look I knew so well. "Frankie," she began. She'd already picked this up from Max. Practically everyone had taken to calling me Frankie. I felt like I was three years old. "Frankie, darling," she explained. "*Jersey* is the name of a place in England. That's why they call ours *New* Jersey. It's just like New York. They're named after places in *old* England. That's why they call them *New*."

"Like New Hampshire," put in Uncle Charlie, who was busy tearing his cocktail napkin into pieces, then rolling these into balls and lining them along the edge of the table.

"Or New*Ark*?" I suggested.

My mother ignored us both. "That's how come they call the whole place *New* England," she concluded triumphantly.

"The only thing I could never figure out," said Uncle Charlie, nudging one ball a little closer to the next, "is the *other* states. How come they don't call it New Massachusetts? New Vermont? New Rhode Island—"

"Oh, shut up, Uncle Charlie," snapped my mother. She turned her attention to Max. "We were among the First Families." Max nodded, looking appropriately impressed.

"Mom," I responded—this must have been a new innovation, such as she came up with every decade or so—"The First Families of *New Jersey?*"

"It's a lovely sunset, isn't it?" said my aunt Clara, perhaps hoping to change the subject.

No one seemed to notice.

We adjourned to the dining area, a mirrored alcove that adjoined the living room. Over dinner, a turkey-and-potatoes fest worthy of the Founding Fathers, the conversation turned to a subject I'd been successfully avoiding all evening: me.

"My nephew Frederick is in the corrugated-box business," my mother was saying to Magee, while Uncle Charlie delivered such dinnertime inanities as "Slap a ham on Omaha, pals," and "Kayak salad, Alaska yak" to anyone who would listen.

"You wouldn't have dreamed it, probably," said Mom, "but it's a million-dollar enterprise. I mean, just think of how many boxes you see around you each day. They're everywhere!" She sighed. "It's so important to have a . . . purpose for your life." She looked at me pointedly.

To which Uncle Charlie remarked, "Go hang a salami, I'm a lasagna hog!"

"Uncle Charlie?" my mother said in a warning tone, lifting one eyebrow in that "Don't you have something to say to Frank" signal I knew so well.

Oh no, I thought, *here we go.*

"Er, yes." Uncle Charlie swiveled in his chair abruptly to face me. "You've got to make your mark upon the world! Seize the . . . hmmm . . . carpe diem . . . what is it he's supposed to seize?"

"The fish?" ventured my aunt Clara. "No, that can't be it. . . ."

My mother rolled her eyes, sipping at her wine. "The *day*, Uncle Charlie. Frankie's got to seize the day. Just like our Frederick did with his boxes."

"He seized the day with his boxers?" Aunt Clara hadn't had two glasses of wine back-to-back in at least thirty years, and her eyes widened behind her trifocals at the notion.

"*Boxes,* Clara, he seized it with his boxes." My mother turned to me. "Now, darling, listen to me, how *is* your book going?"

"Fine, fine," I said, in a feeble attempt to avert the cataclysm.

"So you've been out here now for . . ."

"Eight months, one week, and three days," put in my aunt.

My mother leaned back in her seat, appearing to relax. But this was merely a feint to throw me off balance. "This"— she nodded to Magee—"is a very fine claret."

"It's one of our favorites," said Magee. She refilled my mother's glass for the third or fourth time. "Anyone care for more potatoes?"

"So, you all met at Boscoe, from what I understand?" My mother might have looked like she'd been diverted, but she was tacking determinedly toward the goalposts.

"Yep." Max waved the turkey leg he was holding like a scepter. "Frankie is one of our oldest and most trusted friends."

I felt unaccountably guilty at this remark.

"Frank is just a *love,* that's all I can say about him." Magee smiled radiantly.

Well, maybe not so unaccountably.

"And you're both writers?" Mom was making a line drive for the end zone.

"Yes," they said as one, though Magee turned to me with a shrug and lifted her eyebrows, as though to say in her case that meant "more or less."

"So perhaps you might answer a question," my mother persisted. "Do you think Frank has real talent?"

"Frankie here is one of the most talented unknown writers I know," Max said. "Why, once he gets that novel finished——"

"Which," said my mother, "is exactly my point. Tell me, how long does it generally take to finish a novel?"

"A *novel?*" Max was clearly beginning to realize that the direction the conversation had taken was not a random one. "Why, that's an enormous undertaking. My first one took . . . let's see"—I could see him scrambling in his head, trying to calculate a favorable response—"over a year."

"Arrgh," I groaned audibly, but nobody was paying me any mind. They'd all commenced the family tradition of talking about me as though I wasn't there.

"But a truly *complex* novel . . ." Magee gave Max a poke with her elbow. "Flaubert, for instance, took six years to write *Madame Bovary*——"

"Wasn't that a dirty book?" put in Aunt Clara.

"I read an article," my mother carried on, "that said ninety-five percent of all successful writers make it before the age of thirty."

". . . but a virtual epic," Max was still trying to save the situation, "like Frankie's trying to write . . ."

The next half hour deteriorated into a generalized Frank-bashing harangue, refereed by my mother but launched into with some vigor by Aunt Clara and Uncle Charlie as well:

"How's he going to make a living?"

"He needs to find a nice girl and settle down."

"Quit being such a dreamer."

"Get his feet on the ground!"

"Marriage!"

"Children!"

"Money!"

"Money!"

"Money!"

The barrage built to its predictable climax: a veritable oration by my uncle Charlie on the many rewards of the dry-cleaning business, a topic he'd no doubt been primed to pursue long before landing at LAX.

I tried to defend myself by various means: claiming allergies to cardboard dust and dry-cleaning fluids . . . a constitutional inability to be anywhere by 9:00 A.M.——I was finally delivered from my torment only by the entry of Magee's calico cats, Leon and Vronsky, whose curiosity had at last overcome their aloofness, leading them to trot coolly in from the hallway as though arriving fashionably late at a party in their honor.

"Leon," exclaimed Magee. "Vronsky. My darlings!"

This greeting had the predictable effect of provoking them to complete indifference. Leon settled into position and began washing himself with his tongue, while Vronsky sauntered casually over in the direction of Aunt Clara.

"Was it a cat I saw?" remarked Uncle Charlie, who, having discharged his responsibilities, was reverting blessedly to form. "Taco cat!"

Aunt Clara held out one hand to fend off Vronsky, who was at her feet ogling the most direct route to her lap. "I'm allergic," she laughed apologetically. "They always know, don't they?"

Vronsky sat and pretended to be deeply interested in cleaning the toes of his right paw.

My aunt relaxed. She turned to Max and, in her new claret-induced state of volubility, brought up the other subject I'd been trying to avoid all evening: "So what kind of books do you write?"

I scanned the room, searching for the nearest large piece of furniture to hide myself beneath. But Max acquitted himself admirably. "I write about love," he said. "The only adventure in the modern world!"

"Love, and women's bod——" Magee began, with a snort. But fortunately she was cut off by a loud "Oof!" from Aunt Clara, as twelve pounds of calico cat flesh landed in her lap.

"Bad kitty!" Clara shoved Vronsky to the floor with surprising vigor. She rummaged in her bag for a tissue, groped at her polka-dot scarf, and finally grabbed her napkin. "I——I——ooh. I——I——aaaaahhhhhchooo!"

Vronsky, entirely nonchalantly, went to work on his other paw, while Leon sidled up from the opposite side.

"Vronsky!" said Magee. "Leon. Bad kitties!" This had as much effect on them as had her earlier enthusiastic greeting.

At this point Uncle Charlie, who'd been lost in thought for some time, suddenly reentered the conversation. "A man, a plan, a cat, a canal: Panama!" he said triumphantly.

My mother rolled her eyes and shook her head. "A man, a pain, a mania: Panama," she corrected.

"Hey, that's pretty good!" exclaimed Uncle Charlie, seeming more impressed than rebuffed.

By this point my aunt was sitting on the edge of her chair, sniffling and holding her polka-dot scarf against her face. Every time she glanced away the cats edged closer.

Max moved to eject the beasts at last, grumbling: "Senile felines!"

Dinner was over at last, which meant smoking time. Max and Magee had a special room they called the Smoking Room, but since they smoked all the time, anywhere they wanted, I never could figure out why they felt obliged to have a special room for it. In any case, they rarely used it, and there was no sign of anyone adjourning there now.

I found myself staring, forgetting myself, as Magee shook a Chesterfield nonfilter from her pack—other brands, according to her, yielded no real smoke—and struck a match. She applied the flame to the tip and inhaled luxuriously, lips puckering slightly around the end. Magee smoked with such pleasure it was almost embarrassing to watch, as though you had stumbled upon some intimate, private moment not meant to be witnessed by mere mortals. I'd always hated smoking. But gazing on her at that moment, I wanted to be that cigarette: lifted to those perfect lips, then slowly, utterly consumed.

"What are *you* looking at?" Magee smiled, exhaling a stream of smoke in the direction of Aunt Clara.

I just smiled back at her, hopelessly; but then Uncle Charlie said something funny at the other end of the table and Magee broke the spell by collapsing first into laughter, then one of her coughing fits.

I looked down at my barely touched plate: the frustrated mound of potatoes, the poor repressed turkey leg. There was a ring of peas around the edge of the plate where I'd pushed them, playing with my food. The cabbage was curdling with anxiety.

Uncle Charlie poked at the leftover bones on his plate. "Bird rib," he commented to himself.

Max returned from ejecting the cats. He tossed the end of his tasseled scarf over one shoulder as he settled back into his chair. Then he offered around his cigar case, provoking a stiff but polite recoil from my mother and Aunt Clara, and a wistful shake of the head from my uncle Charlie.

"Puff up!" Uncle Charlie said.

Max proceeded to clip the end off one of his mile-long stogies and light up, relaxing into his seat with one hand on his paunch and a satisfied look on his blocky features.

"You know, I think I'll have one of those too," said

Magee, provoking twin horror-stricken looks from my mother and Clara. "Anybody want this?" she held up her half-finished cigarette. She stubbed it out when she got no response, then reached for the former reptile that served as Max's cigar case. Serenely, Magee clipped the end off one of the thick brown cylinders, placed it between her lips, and lit up too, exhaling a dank-smelling cloud of smoke over the table. The thing looked too large for her mouth, if truth be known; it was almost obscene. The tip glowed red in the dim light.

"I . . . have asthma," Aunt Clara said faintly. She seemed to be growing smaller before my eyes, shrinking gradually into her chair.

Max nodded in sympathy. "Terrible growing older, isn't it?" he puffed. "Why, I once knew a man who had lumbago . . ."

But our hostess just looked over the scene with a benign smile. "It must be so nice," she sighed, "to have a family."

This provoked a notable pause in the conversation, while everyone went through their own private responses. I caught sight of myself in the mirrored wall by the sliding glass door, wearing what I can only describe as a look of utter incredulity.

"Magee and I both lost our parents when we were young." Max broke the silence, his eyes wide and brown and sincere. He puffed at his cigar. "We were brought up in foster homes. It's one thing we have in common." This provoked another lull while everyone tried to figure out what the appropriate response was to such a situation. Even Uncle Charlie was at a loss.

"Today's generation," my aunt Clara said at last, "has almost lost sight of the virtue of family."

"You're absolutely right," agreed Max, and the conversation lurched back into gear.

While everyone else was diverted I turned to Magee. "I never knew that about the foster homes," I said. "I'm sorry."

Magee examined the end of her cigar. "It's O.K.," she said. "It's all behind us now."

"Families are a mixed bag anyway—" I began.

"Oh, but they love you," she said. "Isn't that the important thing?"

After dinner it was time for parlor games, Magee-style.

"O.K." She stood in the living room, surrounded by duplicate Magees reflected from the fireplace wall and mirrors, while Mom, Clara, and Uncle Charlie lined up on the felt sofa like a trio of obedient schoolchildren. Max settled into his Lazy-Guy recliner, and I pulled a chair in from the edge of the dining area. Through the picture window over Magee's shoulder, a crescent moon tilted in the sky like a glass slipper.

"Everyone, at heart," said Magee, "has the nature of an animal. Some are bears, some are mice, some are lions. . . . Now, if you were an animal, what would you be?"

"Not a cat!" giggled Aunt Clara, who, having started into her third glass of claret, was beginning to discover a whole new dimension to life.

"Do not start at rats to nod!" answered my uncle Charlie, predictably.

"I think I'd have to be . . . a wolf," responded Max. He poured himself another tumblerful of cognac.

"Fitting," said Magee, with seeming nonchalance.

This provoked another moment of silence.

"How about you, Mrs. Matthews?" Magee asked my mother, who was moving beyond her distinctly tipsy phase into the uncontrollable hiccuping zone.

"I think," my mother replied, "I'd like to be an owl."

"An owl?" asked Aunt Clara. "Why?"

"I don't know," said my mother. "Maybe I just don't give a hoot!" This tickled her no end, and she giggled off into a spasm of hiccups.

"If I were an animal," said Magee, "I'd like to be some sort of flying beast, like a dragon—but utterly transparent, so that everything inside me was exposed, nothing hidden: a huge transparent winged beast, with a long whiplike tail, slicing across the heavens . . ."

"Very dramatic," hiccuped my mother.

"What about me?" I asked. "What should I be?"

"You?" Max had so far this evening been exceptionally well-behaved, but he was beginning to exhibit the signs of being exceptionally well-oiled. "You're a . . . sort of guppy, I'd say." For some reason he seemed to find this inordinately funny, and he kept chuckling and opening and closing his mouth in a fishlike fashion, which irritated me no end.

Magee, however, rescued me from my torment. "I presume we're all acquainted with that Emily Dickinson poem, where she calls the guppy the Noblest of Fish?"

"Emily Dickinson said that?" responded my mother.

Max, sipping at his cognac, narrowed his eyes suspiciously. Everyone else was too surprised to say anything at all.

Whatever the tension was between Max and Magee, it appeared to be escalating. It finally came to a head when Magee, dishing up a late dessert in the living room, scooped herself out a second portion of ice cream.

"What's that about, babe?" Max, sitting in his leather recliner, lifted his eyebrows. "You don't usually have seconds."

Magee paused with the spoon halfway to her mouth. "Seems these days," she responded, "the plumper you are, the more sex appeal you've got."

"What's that supposed to mean?"

The two of them stared at each other; then Magee turned away and began talking to my aunt Clara.

Max got to his feet and left the room.

A while later I wandered off to use the bathroom. On the way I passed Max standing in an odd nook in the hallway, a leftover from some remodeling project, that had a window looking out over the patio. He didn't say a thing to me, just kept gazing into nothingness in an apparent trance, cigar in hand, mumbling to himself as though repeating a mantra. I could have been wrong, but as I went by I thought I heard him saying:

"Dark Indian women in bright saris, like shadows wrapped in sun . . . Bright Nordic women, blond as summer, with tiny gaps between their front teeth . . ."

My mother's condition was progressing quickly; by the time I returned she'd moved from her uncontrollable hiccuping phase to the realm of deep thought. She and Magee were sitting on the brown sofa, deeply into a conversation about quantum physics, a subject my mother knew nothing about.

"So the quasars—" Mom was saying, sipping at a fresh glass of claret.

I couldn't help interrupting. "Mom, you mean the quarks. Quarks are subatomic particles; quasars are exploding stars."

"Well, there are quarks in the quasars, aren't there?" she said.

I couldn't find anything to say to that.

Aunt Clara, meanwhile, who was onto her fourth glass of claret, had taken over the recliner. She kept rocking it back and forth so the footrest popped out, giggling every time it happened, delighted as a child. "Nine months," she was saying, as though to herself. "That's what I told him. After all, that's how long it takes to make a baby. And if you can't finish it in that time, then you're not going to . . ."

Uncle Charlie had plopped down to a cross-legged position on the floor, from which he wistfully eyed Max's cigar case on the glass coffee table. He inched his hand toward it from time to time, then pulled it away, then inched toward it again.

The dialogue between Alice and the Cheshire Cat from *Alice's Adventures in Wonderland* kept running through my head: "We're all mad here. I'm mad, you're mad . . .""How do you know I'm mad?" "You must be, or you wouldn't have come here."

My mother had reverted to her favorite subject. I heard her voice float up from the vicinity of the couch: "Jersey *was* one of the original thirteen states . . ." she was insisting. "Or maybe it was the fourteenth?"

All of a sudden Magee turned to address the room: "We human beings . . . why are we all so afraid of each other?"

Everyone swiveled around to look at her, but nobody appeared to have any idea what she was talking about. After a moment the conversation resumed. But from the opposite end of the room my eyes found Magee's. They met, or so I imagined, in a long gaze of mutual understanding.

The evening sort of fell apart after that. It started when Max, who'd since rejoined us, was in the midst of a conversation on the couch with Uncle Charlie. "Fictions, see?" he was saying. "It's all just fictions. I don't mean only us writers, I mean everyone—"

All at once he stopped in mid-sentence, stood up, and clapped his palm to his forehead. "I just remembered! We have to move the clocks forward for daylight savings time."

"It's not tonight," put in Magee decisively, from across the room. "It's tomorrow."

"Isn't it Saturday night they do it?" said Uncle Charlie.

"And it's back, not forward," Magee added.

"No," insisted Max. "It's forward in the fall . . ."

"Why would they call it *daylight* savings time," put in Aunt

Clara, "if it happens at night?" She plunked the recliner suddenly backward, emitting a startled "Oh!"

I glanced at the clock on the mantelpiece, as though it could tell me the answer. The mirrored face on the thing had always made me uneasy, for if you looked at the right angle you saw the hands ticking their way across your own features.

"I think it's supposed to happen Sunday morning," I said.

"No, it's forward," said Max, his eyes growing larger than ever under the conceptual strain, "it's got to be, because if you think about it . . ."

"The revolution of the earth," my mother agreed, nodding.

"Fall forward, spring up!" announced Aunt Clara, bouncing back to upright position.

"And it's not to *begin* daylight savings time," said Magee. "It's to end it."

"No, Magee," Max was persisting, "I'm sure it's—"

"You're sure of everything, aren't you?" said Magee. "Well, maybe you should try *not* being so entirely sure for a change." With that she stalked out of the room.

Max looked around, his eyes big and helpless. "Excuse me," he said, and followed her.

"So what time *is* it?" asked Aunt Clara.

Max and Magee retired down the hall to their bedroom, where they could fight in relative privacy. I could only hear disconnected bits of the exchange through the wall, that I wasn't at all sure I was deciphering correctly:

"Frolicking with hippopotamuses—"

(might have been: "prophecies of Nostradamus")

"It's a business thing—"

(might have been: "meretricious fling")

"Her husband has a chain of bookstores—"

(might have been: "hustling and the shame of divorce").

The conflict built in intensity, as these things tend to do, until there was a series of shouts and crashes, followed by various moaning, crying, and making-up noises—and finally, the predictable, rhythmic thunking of a bed against the wall.

"Sexes!" exclaimed my uncle Charlie. "Party boobytrap."

My mother kept cocking her head and glancing down the hallway. Every once in a while she opened her mouth to say something but thought better of it.

"Have they gone to sleep, then?" my aunt Clara put forth, then sneezed. With that, she moved to the couch and nodded off.

My uncle switched on the TV.

I was sitting beside the table at the edge of the dining area. Magee's smile was still etched in lipstick upon her cup. I looked over at her cigar butt, lying there in the ashtray. It, too, bore a faint pink ring of lipstick, the clear impression of Magee's lips. I wondered vaguely whether lip prints were unique, like fingerprints.

If so, there was one unique set of prints stamped upon my soul.

We waited around a while, the news playing on the TV in the background. My mother and I sat on the sofa beside my sleeping aunt Clara, while Uncle Charlie played with the remote control from his pilot's seat in Max's recliner. It was the usual thing: earthquakes in Patagonia, flooding in the Amazon. The threat of war. There were riots in central Los Angeles—the cities were burning.

My mother, as always when she got tipsy, wanted to talk—and cry. "Oh, Frankie," she sniffed, "what are you going to do with yourself?"

"I don't know, Mom."

She stared at the television. Smoke was rising from some Middle Eastern city. "It *looks* like the end of the world," she said. "But I can't imagine the apocalypse would come now, would it? It would never happen on a Saturday."

Aunt Clara, waking, looked around and burped gently. "Oh," she said, "you all drank me under the table!"

"*I* roamed under it as a tired, nude Maori," responded Uncle Charlie.

Finally I took the keys to the Ocelot, left Max and Magee a note, and got us out of there. I figured if they needed to go somewhere they could use the Mercedes, if it was working, or call a taxi.

On the way home I heard my mother, who was moving into her post-philosophical affectionate phase, say from the backseat, "You know, Uncle Charlie, Magee's right. You *are* clever."

"Flee to me, remote elf!" responded my uncle Charlie, tenderly, and took her in his arms.

Home at last, the three of us carried in Aunt Clara, who was passed out for good this time, and put her to bed. While my mother monopolized the bathroom, Uncle Charlie pulled me aside.

"You know what, Frankie?" He clapped me on the back. "I *like* it out here. I think you're doing just fine. And that Max—what a terrific fella!"

I tried repeating his phrase to myself backward, but it came out, in part, "Allef cifirret atahw xam taht dna."

This was no palindrome. He must have meant it.

The next afternoon, as I was preparing to drive back over the hills to Malomar to return the car, I got a call from Magee. She didn't even mention the Ocelot.

"Sorry about last night—" she began.

"You're forgiven," I said. "In any case, you've accomplished a valuable mission. They're headed back home tomorrow, no doubt never to return."

"I *did* enjoy meeting them," said Magee. Her voice had a wistful edge to it. "But you know, Frank, Max and I were thinking. We've got the garage apartment, and there's no one living in it. We need someone to watch over the place sometimes when we're away, and your time with your aunt is running out, and . . . Well, why don't you just move in? Rent-free, of course."

I'd spent my life fleeing the ordinary, the commonplace; and Max and Magee's life still seemed to me at that point to exhibit a sort of special glow, a lustre—an aura that was almost mystical.

How could I refuse?

"Sure," I agreed.

And so it was decided.

7

In Which Magee and I Are Left Home Alone

 *I KNOW it's not right to worship a woman, but there it is, undeniable. She is a higher power, the all-pervading Almighty. She is Jehovah and she is Krishna. She is Zoroaster and Jesus, Hera, Athena, Artemis. I can't look on her without being blinded.*

I've studied the Upanishads, the Kabbalah, and the Koran. I've pondered the Torah, the New Testament, the Bhagavad Gita. But now I ponder only Magee. My only God is Magee. Magee is the Great Center. Magee is the One.

As you can see, my novel was continuing to progress. It was even beginning to acquire a certain mystical theme— though I hadn't gotten around yet to changing the names of the characters. But the main thing was that writing had become, once again, something I needed.

That part about the sacred texts of the world was true. But since I'd moved into my garage apartment at Malomar, I'd taken on a new course of study. I was studying Magee. Almost despite myself, I found myself examining her daily habits with an attention that might almost be called compulsive. Actually, it *was* compulsive. I studied her eating habits, drinking habits, resting habits . . . mating rituals. Unlike a man of science, however, I couldn't claim to be utterly objective. I wanted to climb inside her soul and live there. Still, a series of conclusions was beginning to emerge—enough that it had become possible to compile a sort of report for myself, or at any rate, a list of observations:

1) Magee was constantly changing her makeup, or the style or color of her hair, or something about herself, on at least a weekly basis. It was like being around a human kaleidoscope. I couldn't figure Max's obsession about bedding every type of woman in the world. Magee *was* every type of woman in the world.

2) Magee was not afraid to use her sex appeal to get what she wanted. Once she and I were returning from an errand when we were pulled over on the Coast Highway by a couple of big, swaggering cops. "Seventy-five miles an hour?" exclaimed Magee, fluttering her eyelashes at the leather-clad he-men like a 1950's movie starlet. "Why, ahhhh had no idea!" The icicles of their eyes melted. They not only drove off without ticketing

us, they tipped their hats in parting and said, "You take it easy now, little lady. And have a good afternoon."

"What did you do that for?" I said. It was a side of her I hadn't seen before, and I was amazed, if a little appalled, to see it in action.

"They let us go, didn't they?" Magee shrugged. "If that didn't work, I was going to burst into tears."

3) She was given to brief, sharp enthusiasms. I rose one morning and came into the main house for coffee, as was my habit, to find Magee already bustling about, cleaning out a spare room that had always been used for storage.

"What are you doing?" I asked.

"I'm setting up a studio. I'm going to take up weaving."

By the time she had the room prepared, she'd lost interest. The mail-order loom she'd sent for sat there, half-assembled and surrounded by bright reels of unraveling yarn, for the rest of the time I lived in Malomar.

4) Magee's Daily Activities: Despite Magee's denials, she did write, and generally on a daily basis—although she was secretive about this pursuit and explained it away by saying she was "keeping track of her dreams." She also read ravenously. It was not unusual for her to have three books going at once: say, Turgenev, Djuna Barnes, and Philip K. Dick. One year, she told me, she'd read all the Nobel Prize–winners as far back as the prize went. Then she'd started in on the Pulitzers.

She continued to play piano occasionally and supervised the upkeep of the house and grounds—which, although a large job, seemed hardly a sufficient match for her talents. She watched classic black-and-white movies on their state-of-the-art video system for hours.

I eventually came to realize that she spent much of her time doing nothing at all.

But she did it so well!

As she put it: "There's just no *time* for anything else."

5) Husband and Wife Together: Their fights were monumental, apocalyptic: screams and inarticulate wailing; thrown ashtrays and smashed liquor bottles; dead butts and whiskey strewn across the furniture—and then, by some strange form of mutual consent, they'd retire to the bedroom, from which would issue screams and inarticulate wailing. . . .

These were phenomena that soon passed, like electrical storms, leaving the air clear and sharp with the tang of ozone. Still, occurrences appeared to be increasing in frequency—at this point, once or twice a week.

All this was just a start on what really deserved, I thought, a lifetime of study. But like all truly beautiful women, Magee evaded analysis; she was a whole that could not be reduced to the sum of her parts. She was, finally, ineffable, mysterious, and ungraspable.

Still, I was headed into dangerous waters, I knew. My loyalty to Max was my only life preserver—and a rather leaky one, at that.

It was crazy, but I couldn't take my mind off her. Magee's

beauty had pierced something inside me, and the hook was barbed. I knew I'd never be able to get it out.

At last, when Max was away on an advance tour for *The Telltale Breast,* the moment came that I craved and dreaded. I was alone in my apartment, just before dusk, halfheartedly trying to meditate again, when the phone rang.

"Hey, Frank, whatchoo doing?" Magee's voice came over the line, sweeter than wine.

"Not much," I said. "Sitting around, trying to meditate."

If I'd spoken the truth I'd have said, "Sitting around, dreaming of you."

"Max has an interview on the Bob Cleverman show tonight. Do you want to come down and watch, maybe play a game of backgammon afterward?"

I walked into the living room to find her sitting before an overflowing ashtray, a crumpled Chesterfield pack empty on the coffee table, and a drink in her hand. There was a book facedown on the glass surface: the second volume, I think, of Proust. She was just about to light another cigarette. The place was literally filled with smoke.

"Jesus," I said, throwing open the sliding door that led to the patio, for it was a balmy enough evening in the mild Malomar fall. "Don't you know the Surgeon General recommends you take in some air with your smoke, at least five times a day?" Magee just shrugged helplessly, smiling, and lit the next in the chain.

She was sitting on the brown felt couch, wearing blue jeans and a white lacy top, one cat snoozing beside her and the other draped loosely over the back of the couch behind her head, purring so loudly I could hear it from halfway across the room. As anyone would be, I thought, if they had the privilege of sleeping so close to Magee.

Magee's bare feet were propped on the glass of the coffee table, beside a centerpiece of flowers from the garden and some unlit candles. I don't think I've mentioned Magee's feet before; but if anyone should be laboring under the misapprehension that this woman was too perfect to actually exist, let us consider them: pudgy rectangles of flesh with squared-off toes, they seemed stuck onto her body as an afterthought, as though God had exhausted Himself in creating such a vision of beauty and, not having the energy to finish the job off properly, grabbed a spare set that happened to be lying about and put them in place. Magee seemed alternately amused and embarrassed by them. Rumor had it that she coated them with Vaseline at night and slept with her socks on to keep them soft. Today the nails were painted lavender.

She patted the sofa next to her with the hand that wasn't holding the cigarette. "Sit down, Frank. Make yourself at home." She took another drag and I saw the ash drop to the cushion, whose brown felt seemed to simply sigh and absorb it. Perhaps, I thought, that's why she'd kept the sagging sofa all those years, despite Max's protests.

What was it, I often wondered, about Magee and cigarettes? In my memories of her from those years, she is always smoking. It wasn't as though she was one of those smokers who holds a cigarette as a prop or to give her something to do with her hands. She consumed them, one after the next, with a fearsome attention, as though they were the purpose of her life. At a certain point I realized she gave more consistent time and energy to cigarettes than practically anything else. They were the through line of her being, performed again and again with an almost ritualistic repetition. At center, she was an unbroken line of lit cigarettes.

She had once, back at Boscoe, delivered to me a rather incredible monologue on this subject. As I recall, it went something like: "Did you know the lips have more nerve endings than any other part of the body? Think of little kids—they're always putting things to their mouths, kissing the world. When I was a child my parents had to keep everything away from me or I'd put it in my mouth—maybe that's why I'm so attached to smoking. Every few minutes, most of the day, I get to put something to my mouth again and again. . . . But then, if you think about it, that's all we are, really: one long mouth. The whole digestive tract is connected, one continuous tube from lips to anus. So we're always, in a way, kissing our own asses."

Tonight she was drinking Pernod, which I'd never even heard of before. A bottle stood on the table, clear liquid behind sea-green glass. Magee explained it was the same as absinthe, without the wormwood, and quipped: "Absinthe makes the heart grow fonder."

Impossible, in my case—I was operating at peak fondness capacity already.

"Van Gogh used to drink it," Magee said, "and look how well he turned out."

I sat on the couch beside her, opposite to whichever cat was sprawled out on her right—I couldn't tell them apart any more than I could the dogs. She had a second tumbler already on the table beside the ice bucket. Magee plunked a couple of cubes into my glass and poured in a generous dollop of the licorice-smelling liquid, which immediately turned a turbid yellowish color.

"Here's to . . ." She glanced toward the TV, which featured a troupe of happy people frolicking in a field because they'd overcome occasional irregularity. "Well, I guess it ought to be to Max, shouldn't it?"

"To Max," I agreed—with, I must admit, a hint of reluctance. I held up my glass, took a sip of the bittersweet, rather bilious fluid, and settled back to watch the show.

Magee sighed, almost involuntarily, when she saw Max walk onto the set, his stride strong and confident, the band striking up behind him. "Why, he almost looks like the old Max. The man I fell in love with."

"He sure knows how to make an entrance, I'll give him that," I said. "And he's the kind of guy who appreciates having a band to announce it."

Max looked surprisingly good on-screen. Maybe it was the makeup or a trick of the lighting, but he seemed to have shed five years and twenty-five pounds overnight. Even his little round bald spot appeared distinguished.

He'd obviously rehearsed for the event. When Cleverman, after a couple of obligatory jokes about the mightiness of the author's pen, asked how he'd got his start, Max launched in, "I set out as a writer with a simple goal: to wrest one impeccable sentence from the gibberish of experience."

This was followed by one of the longest silences I'd ever heard on a talk show. "Hmm . . ." Cleverman rallied after a minute. "If you succeeded, what would you do?"

Max shrugged. "Write it down and burn it, probably."

That provoked a pretty good laugh from the studio audience, and after that Max had them in the palm of his hand. He talked a little about the source of his inspiration——the condensed answer being: himself. Then he went off on a long tangent about the creative process.

"You know, Bob," he said, "I get this funny feeling sometimes, when I'm working on a book, that the whole thing is already complete in my subconscious mind, and my job is just to uncover it."

Max seemed to be making a bid for being taken more seriously as a writer——something he'd been talking a lot about lately.

"Eh, yes——" Cleverman was attempting to regain control over the interview, but Max just carried right on: "It's as though we writers are archaeologists, and our books are buried cities we must unearth. All we can do is try to uncover them as carefully as possible, knowing that we will inevitably fracture a few metaphors, break a plotline or two——and all the while, our deepest obsessions are lurking beneath the ground, like mummies wrapped in burlap."

"Well," said Cleverman, "I have to admit that after

reading *City of Breasts,* I didn't expect this conversation to be quite so . . . intellectual."

There was laughter, and the band gave a roll-of-the-drums toot of appreciation. But Max had a firm control on the proceedings; just when you thought he was going to plunge headlong into complete pretension, he started sending himself up. "You know, Bob," he said. "Sometimes people think I'm arrogant—as though I want to be God, or I'm operating under the assumption I *am* God or something. . . . It's not that. It's just that if anything ever happened to him I'd want to be considered as a stand-in."

After that the show was Max's. He concluded, believe it or not, by reciting from memory the closing lines to *City of Breasts:*

> *I remember Los Angeles; the buildings thrusting up rigidly, like pillars of salt into the haze. Smog hanging over the city like a cloud of cigarette smoke. The tangle of freeways, strewn about everywhere like cast-off stockings.*
>
> *I remember. I remember. I remember Los Angeles.*

There must have still been a minute or two to fill before the station break, because Cleverman asked him one last question:

"So what will you do next?"

"I don't know." Max shrugged. "Maybe I'll start a new religion. I'll call it . . . the Church of *Me*. Hey, that's kind of catchy, no?"

Then came the theme music, and Max shaking Cleverman's hand and grinning and clapping him on the back, followed by a commercial for Permo-Stick denture adhesive.

Magee and I had to give old Max a round of applause after that. Whatever anybody might think of him, he hadn't missed a beat.

The theme song was playing over the credits; it was a jazz standard, one of my favorites, called "Takin' My Sweet Time." And as I sat there listening, I had a revelation. Could it be, I wondered, that *every* artist, no matter their level of talent, had more or less the same creative experience? That the most insipid Top 40 hitmaker felt every bit as inspired as Bobby Zipperman did when he composed "Gather No Moss"—and being inside Max Peterson when he wrote *City of Breasts* wasn't all that different from being inside F. Scott Fitzgerald when he was composing *The Great Gatsby*, or Faulkner when he was writing *Absalom, Absalom!*?

I don't always know what I feel. Sometimes I look inside and draw a big blank, like I'm floating in empty space. In fact one of my brief—you might say momentary—love interests had given me the nickname "Blank Frank." But I'd noticed early on that Magee was a creature of moods, and she wasn't the kind of person who accommodated them to the presence of others. Tonight, she carried a lingering, melancholic thoughtfulness—which for me, predictably, only had the effect of accentuating her loveliness.

After the applause from our own Malomar studio audience settled down, Magee sat quietly, blond strands spilling around her face, staring off into nothing. She'd lit the candles on the coffee table once the show ended, and the quivering light brought out the greenness of her eyes.

"When is he coming back?" I asked finally, to keep the silence from getting too uncomfortable.

"Who?"

"Max," I said. "Your husband."

"Oh," Magee answered, as though from a distance. "He's got this mysterious friend Henry he goes to visit anytime he's back East. I never get to meet him, though he phones up once in a while. . . ." She trailed off.

"Is something wrong?"

"I don't know." Magee stared out the east window to where the moon, just past full, was cresting up through the clouds. I could see the surf, far below, gleaming silver, rising and crashing onto the shore. "Did I ever tell you," she said, "that when I met Max I thought he was the handsomest man I'd ever seen?"

I rummaged through the overstuffed closet of memory. Could we possibly be talking about the same Max? I couldn't recall a single occasion, even at age twenty, when Max hadn't been disheveled, enormous, and galumphing—even if, to be fair, he *did* possess a certain primal energy that women seemed to go for. Maybe that was it, I thought—and his big sad eyes, which always made women want to rescue him.

"I remember," Magee was saying, "the first time I went for a drive with him. He had this Alfa Romeo he'd borrowed from his roommate. I guess he thought I was too classy for the hearse. And he was right." She smiled at the recollection. "He was a few years older than me and with the reputation he had, I wouldn't be caught—ha!—dead in it. Anyway, the Alfa broke down, like they always do, stranding us on the side of the highway, traffic whistling past. Max got out, cursing; he was sweating and kicking the tires—and all of a sudden I realized, with a kind of internal amazement: I'm going to marry this guy." She was smiling still, but she shook her head. "If I'd only known what I was getting myself into."

"What do you mean?"

"Oh"—shrugged Magee—"his debts and everything."

"Debts?" The revelation surprised me.

"Come on, Frank. What writer makes enough money to live like we do?" Then she softened. "But that's the American way, isn't it? I had not thought debt had outdone so many . . ."

I had to laugh. So Max was living the same way I was—by borrowing. It was just on a different scale.

Magee had again grown silent.

"What are you thinking?" I asked.

"Imagine if the world were perfect, Frank. If every cigarette was just terrific, and it never made you cough; if every time you drank coffee or ate sugar it perked you up and there was never a crash afterward; if every time you had a few drinks you woke up the next morning feeling fantastic. If every time you loved there was no letdown. . . ."

An hour or so passed in conversation and watching the TV. We'd finished our second glass of Pernod, and I poured us a third.

"This stuff certainly is interesting," I said.

Magee laughed. "Don't you like it?"

"I'd have to say it exists beyond the realm of like or dislike." I held up my tumbler and swirled the yellowy liquid against the candlelight. "What's it made from, anyway?"

"Aniseed. Max put me onto it, of course. You have to imagine yourself in nineteenth-century Paris, guzzling with Gauguin."

The stuff must have been going to my head, because I suddenly found myself asking, "Magee, were you ever with anyone before Max?"

"Are you kidding? Want to hear the list?" Magee didn't wait for my answer. "My first four lovers were all named John. Let's see, there was:

"John #1: He was a cowboy—insisted on wearing his hat even to bed.

"John #2: He was so cheap he used to reuse his dental floss.

"John #3: He was such a control freak he had to consult a manual to tie his shoelaces.

"John #4: He had emotional constipation. He just didn't give a shit.

"Then there was Edward. He was like one of those irritating places on the inside of your mouth you keep biting over and over. And Chuck. He had all the personality of a potted plant. Tim was a monoplegic: paralyzed from the neck up. Rex—I used to call him my favorite patriot, because he was one of the minutemen: never took more than a minute.

"Al. Now, there was an eager beaver. Used to practice the trombone while sitting on the toilet. 'Got to make the best of every moment,' he said. Then there was George. He was like one of those objects that catches your eye at a flea market, but you bring it home and realize it doesn't fit anywhere and it ends up in a corner collecting dust. Dave. He had omniphobia: fear of everything. And Steve. I don't think of him so much as a man—he was more a sort of larva. . . ."

"Wow. And all of these were *before* Max?" As soon as that was out I wished I'd hadn't said it. But then, I'd never drunk Pernod before and I don't think I was dealing with the effects that well—not to mention the intoxicating influence of the company.

Magee gave me a sideways glance. "I'm often astonished at who I fall in love with. Look at Max. He was losing his hair by age twenty-five, he's paunchy, self-obsessed, and a terrible flirt. But I adore him . . . still. Who knows why?" She stubbed out her cigarette, nudging the old butts aside to make room in the ashtray. "But then, I don't want a love that's small enough to understand. I want a love that's so big I'll never get a handle on it."

They both did lists, I realized, Max and Magee. Maybe they weren't so far apart after all. And as for the truthfulness of *her* list—who could tell? I was beginning to think maybe Magee was as good at creating fictions as Max was.

"Listen, Frank," said Magee. "Some men are friends. Some you love. Some you just fuck. And some—well, you're married to them, and that's that."

I was shocked, I don't know why, by her use of the word

fuck. I'd even heard my mother use it once or twice. I didn't have the nerve to ask where, or whether, I might ever fit into any of those categories.

Magee drew her feet up onto the couch and tucked them beneath her. She rubbed at one of the cat's ears as he lay on the couch beside her; maybe it was Vronsky. He yawned and stretched, purring loudly enough that I could feel the vibration through the couch cushion. For the first time in my life I realized it was possible to envy a cat.

"What about you, Frank? Have you ever been in love?"

I watched the candlelight wander over her face.

"Yes," I said. "No. Well, maybe."

She laughed. "You sound like me before I met Max."

I suddenly caught sight of the two of us, reflected back from the mirrored wall of the fireplace. A clump of sandy hair was sticking skyward from the crown of my head. I reached up to smooth it down.

"What are you looking at?" asked Magee.

"Me." I grimaced at my reflection.

"Why the funny face?"

"It's the most appropriate response?" I half-joked.

"Oh, Frank, I think you're quite handsome. You have . . . classic features."

"No one else ever seems to think so."

"Well," said Magee, reaching over to ruffle my head. "Maybe you *could* do something about that haircut. And it's not generally recognized as a crime in the state of California to own more than a single T-shirt. But still, I don't know why none of my friends went for you. Women are silly sometimes."

"So are men."

The TV was still on, playing in the background. As though in response to Max's interview, it had moved on to a documentary about archaeology—Pompeii, and the eruption of Mount Vesuvius.

I knew exactly how that mountain felt.

Magee saw me looking at the screen. "Those heroes of old were all short. Did you know that? They can tell by the armor they've dug up. Brave Ulysses, Achilles, Paris, the whole bunch. They were only five feet tall." Magee was always surprising me with odd bits of information like that.

But I was still thinking about her list. *No wonder she's with Max,* I thought. *He's the best of the lot.*

After a while, the talk turned to the subject of happiness.

"I know I *ought* to be able to be happy," Magee said, "but I can never seem to manage it. There seems to be so much more opportunity for sadness. You know what I mean?"

I knew.

"But then, maybe the problem is, I've never really known what I wanted."

I figured it might be time to lighten the mood. "How about eliminating the things you *don't* want?" I suggested. "A dish of cold oatmeal?"

"No," she answered. "I don't want that."

"A male aardvark in rut?"

"I think I've already got one of those, thanks."

"A lifetime subscription to *Junior Miss* magazine?"

"Frank, this is going to take all night." But she had to smile. "Let's face it. I've never been satisfied with a thing in my life. Maybe that's just how I'm built."

She leaned back into the couch, stretched her arms over her head, arched her back.

"I have a nice body, don't I?" she said suddenly.

I was experiencing a lot of things that night that I wasn't sure how to respond to.

"Why, of course you do," I said awkwardly. "The best." I could feel my ears burning, the skin of my face go hot. The scent of her, as she sat beside me on the couch, was over-whelming: smoke and cinnamon, Pernod and cloves, a musky tang of perfume. It was like being inside a spice shop.

"Sometimes," she said, "I think Max has entirely forgotten."

I watched as she leaned forward again and tapped her cig-arette against the edge of the ashtray. How many times had she repeated that gesture? Countless times, times beyond measure. And what did it mean? Absolutely nothing.

"Magee," I said, "what do you want to be when you grow up?"

Magee answered sadly: "A saint."

I don't know whether it was Magee or me who suggested the piano, but it seemed a perfect way to round off that evening, with its atmosphere of mild melancholy and the moon rising over the water. Perhaps a more intriguing ques-tion is who suggested we carry the candles to the music room to create the appropriate mood. But I don't remember that either.

"So, why did you give up performing?" I asked as Magee

settled onto the bench in front of her white Steinway grand. She placed her candle on the ledge above the keyboard.

Magee had played piano from an early age, somehow managing to sustain the activity through high school and a number of unpleasant foster homes. Or maybe, from what she said, it was the piano that had sustained her. Until she'd had what she described as a sort of breakdown during one of her first recitals at Boscoe.

"Performing was what I'd always dreamed of," she said, the glow of the candle rising and falling against her features. "But I felt so exposed out there, Frank, alone on that enormous stage with everyone listening. . . . It was as though this great, silent weight started pressing down on me, crushing my hands against the keys, crushing the music out of the air. At a certain point I looked down and I could see my fingers moving over the keyboard, the pattern of white and black—but I couldn't hear a thing. It was as though the notes were going out there into a void and being swallowed up."

I watched the candlelight on her face and imagined the scene: Magee's passion against the tomblike silence of the concert hall, all the men in coats and ties. "I felt like I was going to throw up, or suffocate, or die. I jumped up, slammed down the piano lid, and left the stage. I've never played publicly since."

But that night she played for me—Chopin, Debussy, Satie's Gnossiennes and Gymnopédies, Beethoven's exquisitely difficult Piano Sonata Number 32. This was a moment I'd imagined countless times since I'd first seen her that night at Boscoe. She'd lost none of her ability to wring feeling from sound: the music was by turns melancholic, thrilling, impishly playful, gorgeous. It tugged at places inside me I hadn't even known were there. Everything was much as it had been that night: the hair tumbling across her face, the cigarette burning in the ashtray, the drink vibrating in its glass. The candlelight quivered over the perfection of her features and sent shadows dancing into all the corners of the room. But I had the strangest sense come upon me as I sat listening: as though the moment, even as I was witnessing it, was a memory; and at the same time I was at the center of it, there was another "I" waiting somewhere in the future, watching, remembering.

Magee finished, rising from the bench, and curtsied for my solitary but vigorous applause. Then she lifted the candle and paused to examine herself in a full-length, old-fashioned looking glass that stood in a corner of the room. She stopped and looked, turned this way and that and smoothed her jeans over her hips, before announcing: "My butt's too big, isn't it?"

I really didn't know what I was supposed to say to that. *Well, hardly.* Or, *Actually it's a rather marvelous butt, if you want to know my opinion.* But that seemed too intimate a thing to say to somebody else's wife. Instead I joked: "All humans have big butts. It's what separates us from lower forms of life, such as centipedes and grasshoppers."

"Hmmph," said Magee, without laughing.

She excused herself to use the bathroom and was gone a long time—so long I started to feel worried. After hunting all over I finally found her in her dressing room. I guess she must have had quite a bit to drink by that time, because she was looking at her reflection in the mirror and repeating in a dreamy tone, as though to herself:

"Fading, fading . . ."

"Magee," I said, "are you all right?"

She didn't even look around when I stepped up behind her. "We're all fading, Frank."

"What?" I felt stupid saying it, since I'd heard her perfectly well. But how are you supposed to respond to something like that? It took me a while to realize she was doing her Blanche DuBois routine—but even so, it seemed she was serious.

"At the height of the bloom, you can see the end coming." She smiled at herself in the mirror—more of a grimace, really, though to me it was still a lovely grimace. "See this crease at the edge of my lip? I won't be able to notice exactly when it happens, but one day it will be there even when I'm not smiling. And more creases will come from the corners of my eyes, and here in the middle of my forehead where I frown, and it will all just keep pulling down and down—until one day it'll collapse and I won't be beautiful anymore."

With that, to my astonishment, she burst into tears.

"Oh Frank," she said, "I'm nothing but a fading rose . . . in some flamenco dancer's mouth." The image ought to have been hilarious, but at that moment there was nothing funny about it. My hands fought against each other like airborne birds, unable to decide whether to settle on her shoulders.

"The years," she sobbed, "they just tick by—what's going to happen to me when I'm not young and beautiful anymore?"

I didn't answer. I'd been young for so long I couldn't imagine being any other way.

"Cigarette," she said suddenly. "I left my cigarettes by the piano."

Back on the brown sofa, I lit one for her, my hand shaking a little as I held the match.

"Thank you," she sniffled, puffing out smoke and waving it away with her free hand. "'Ahhh have always depended on the kindness of strangers.'"

She was doing Blanche DuBois again. I suddenly caught sight of her image in the mirrored wall by the fireplace; reflected into the gilt-framed mirror on the opposite wall, it was thrown back to the mirror above the mantelpiece, and back yet again: surrounding me were a dozen images of Magee, like one of Picasso's refracted women, waving around her cigarette, blowing out smoke. Who *was* she? Take away the house, the parties, the glamour and glitter. What if she had to work nine to five? If she had to clean her own home? Would she still be Magee? Would I still love her?

The Magee that existed in the flesh was starting to seem a lot more complicated than the one in my mind ever was.

As she pulled at her cigarette her eyes looked wild, a bit frightened—as though she'd just woken up and found herself living here in this world and had no idea what to do about it.

I sat there, watching her. She stubbed out her spent cigarette, lit a fresh one, and drew heroically on it. In my mind's eye I saw her lungs filled with ash, withering up like old leaves.

"Frank," she asked, after she'd settled down a bit, "who's your favorite writer?"

"Nabokov. Who's yours?"

She almost said something, then didn't. What she ended up saying was, "Max, of course."

She must have seen a look pass across my face, because she said, "O.K., I know maybe it's not the highest literature. But you've got to admit there's a certain—primeval vitality about it."

If cavemen wrote novels, I thought.

"And nobody else ever wrote a book about *me.*"

Nobody else you know about.

"Frank," she said suddenly, as though seeing into my mind. "Can I read *your* novel sometime? I'd like to."

"Well, sure," I said. "Maybe. I might have to do a little revision to get it into shape."

"But what's it about?"

"Oh . . . love, life, the usual things."

"You're being awfully mysterious." She brushed a few blond strands away from her face. The crying fit had softened her, and she was doing her emanating trick again, seeming to exude light.

I reached over to pet Vronsky, if that's who it was, lying between us on the couch. He got up and slunk away. *Cats,* I thought. *They're nothing if not predictable.*

"Tell me the name of it, at least," she persisted.

"The Finished Man," I said, to my surprise. I hadn't known that before. I'd just discovered the title that moment.

The candles were burning low, and Magee was getting more tipsy than I'd ever seen her. I was feeling pretty bleary myself. It was way past my usual bedtime, but I couldn't bear to miss an instant with her. We were half-watching a program about the fiscal policies of presidents. The commentator said something about the "dribble-down" theory of economics, and all of a sudden Magee said:

"*He* dribbles down my leg at night."

"What?" I replied. "Who does?"

"Max. When he comes back from the bathroom. He rolls over and snuggles up to me afterward and I can feel him dribbling down my leg."

She seemed to be expecting a response, but I had no idea what it should be.

Magee looked at me. "Let's smoke one of Max's cigars."

We did, passing it back and forth between us on the couch. The thick, sour-smelling smoke spiraled upward above our heads. I'd never had a cigar before, and the smoke made my head spin. Or something, at least, was making my head spin.

"Magee," I said, "is it *really* true that you don't write anymore?" I'd been wanting to work the conversation around to this all night.

"I write . . . sometimes," she shrugged, seemingly content to let it stop there.

"I remember your writing from back at Boscoe. Magee, it's better than Max's. Why aren't you doing something with it?"

"I wouldn't want my work to appear out there in public where people could just . . . drool on it. That's Max's job." She looked out the window, maybe at the moon, maybe at nothing. "You know, sometimes I wonder—Max is Max. But who am I?"

Magee passed me the cigar. I took it and puffed at it awk-wardly. I felt like we were kids doing something illicit, having found our way into Dad's private stash. All of a sudden she said: "Frank, what is fate?"

This was a way she had, of asking the most profound ques-tions from out of nowhere. I remembered it from college—how she might turn to you abruptly in the line at McDonald's and ask: "Do you believe in a single, almighty creator?"

My head was feeling awfully thick. "Fate?" I said. "It's—what are you asking, exactly?"

"I mean, like in those Greek plays, where Oedipus is des-tined to kill his father and marry his mother, and no matter how everyone tries to get him out of it, that's exactly what he ends up doing."

"So your point is . . ." The room was filled with a haze of smoke; it had been a long night, and my eyes were stinging.

"Sometimes I think about having children. And it seems like I have a choice. But I wonder if that's an illusion, and whichever I *think* I'm choosing—well, that way's already laid out by fate, and there's not a thing I can do about it."

I wasn't sure I could get my brain to wrap itself around philosophy at that hour. "What about Max?" I said. "Does he want kids?"

"Max and I just don't seem to *do* it much anymore. Ex-cept," she added ruefully, "when we've had a fight."

If I was a certain kind of man, I suppose I'd have known what to say at that point. But I must not be that kind, because I didn't. Still, the drink made me bold enough to ask: "Magee, what are you doing with Max, anyway?"

She was quiet for a moment. "Frank," she said, "you don't know a thing about love."

She stubbed out the cigar and raised the bottle of Pernod with a questioning glance. I shook my head—the weird licorice taste of the stuff was beginning to permeate my entire being.

"How about we get some food instead," I said. "I haven't had dinner, have you?"

She put a finger to her lip. "I can't remember."

Together, we raided the pantry for chips, crackers, cheese. I insisted on including carrots and celery sticks to supplement the usual birdlike portions she consumed.

"You're supposed to have vegetables," I said. "*Real* vegetables, every day. Cigarettes don't count."

We settled into the couch with our picnic; or maybe it would be more accurate to say the couch engulfed us. A teardrop of flame stretched up from the candle that sputtered on the table before us, casting its brightness upon us.

"Frank," she asked, munching a carrot stick, "have you ever had a perfect moment?"

Did this woman never quit? I fought back my weariness again, looked into my heart, gulped—and was gifted, I think, with one of the few truly suave moments of my life.

"Of course," I replied. "Sitting here with you."

This bought me the moment of radiance I'd expected—her smile shone down on me like the sun. Or should I say the moon? Magee had always seemed closer, to me, to the moon. But her smile abruptly faded, as though the lights had been switched off; and to my amazement, she again burst into tears. Once more I found myself at a loss for what to do. Once more my hands fought their aerial battle, trying to decide whether they were going to reach out to her—but the decision was taken away, for Magee launched herself into my arms and collapsed, sobbing on my shoulder.

I felt like I was just learning to surf and ten-foot swells were coming in on me from every side. After a moment of near-panic, my hands settled into place and I sat there for a long time, stroking her hair while she cried.

I don't know how to communicate what I felt. It was torment, all right—an unbearably delicious form of it. There was a throbbing through my flesh and bones, as though my body had become one enormous heart. I felt as though Magee's soul had an invisible line attached to it, the other end of which was tethered to my intestines. Maybe you've heard that Faulkner quote—the one that goes something like: "The only fit subject for literature is the human heart in conflict with itself"?

Well, I was rapidly acquiring a whole lot of subject matter.

It was late, and the moon, now drifting down the inside of the dome to the west, was peering in through the front window, watching us. But I needn't have feared what might follow. Magee was one of those people who build to a particular pitch of passion and intimacy only a few minutes before complete collapse. The window of opportunity was so narrow there was no way to fit through it, even if I'd tried.

Her last words were mumbled: "Frank, maybe one day you can teach me to meditate." With that, she drifted off into slumber.

I sat for a long time and watched her sleep, while a rerun of

Bonnie and Clyde played across the TV screen. She looked so tender, innocent—like a child, I thought. Her hair was in a tousle across the cushion and her makeup was smeared from crying, and her chest rose and fell ever so slightly as she breathed—as though she was just sipping at the air, as though she was so light and free she barely needed to breathe at all.

It was all kind of a relief, if truth be told. To quote Clyde Barrow, I'd never been much of a lover-boy type anyway.

The candles had all burned down. The movie ended and an expert was talking about the threat of war in Abyssinia. The world was falling to pieces, as usual. U.S. troops were massed on the border waiting to go in and take out the current dictator. He was impeding his people's access to petroleum, or something like that. Something had to be done.

I was nodding off myself. After going back and forth on what was the right thing, I decided to leave Magee sleeping there alone.

Dawn was beginning to break.

I slid my shoulder from under her head and slipped a pillow beneath it; she scarcely stirred. I was feeling kind of angry, to tell you the truth—at the world, at myself—at Magee too, though I couldn't have said exactly why. I'd had my perfect moment, I told myself. Now it was time to give up this madness once and for all. The last thing I did was put her earring that I'd been carrying around in my pocket on the coffee table. I figured she'd think she'd left it there herself.

But once I was out-of-doors, I didn't feel like sleeping. The sun was about to come up and there was a fresh breeze coming in off the water. Instead, I went down to the beach and set out looking for the secret alcove. The tide was low, and I ended up walking for miles.

But I couldn't find it.

By the time I got back, the sun was fully risen. I passed Jesus, already toiling away on the garden, and we exchanged waves. My garage apartment felt stifling, even with the windows open. The breeze had faded, and the sun streamed relentlessly through my windows, which I hadn't gotten around to getting curtains for yet. It was like living in a greenhouse. There hadn't been an honest cloud in sight for months. I lay down on my bed, on top of the covers, at a loss for anything else to do—it was just too hot, and I was too worn out. It felt odd, lying there above the garage where the Trojan Hearse had been quartered for so long; as though I were living, somehow, atop Max's conquests.

And, in a way, I guess I was.

As I lay there, half-dozing, I had a vision. In my mind's eye I saw the enormous, spread-eagled sprawl of LA, as though the entire city had gotten drunk and fallen on its face—that whole humongous spread of interlocking, sun-broiled highways, like an enormous net, drawing in around me, trapping, enclosing me . . .

Rain! I thought, half-surfacing out of my doze. *Doesn't it ever rain here?*

It wasn't long before it did—and then it didn't stop.

8

In Which I Undertake a Small Investigation

IN ASIA there is a type of monkey trap that is made out of a hollowed-out coconut shell, fastened to the ground. A hole is cut in the top of it and a piece of food is placed inside. The hole is just wide enough for the monkey to reach its paw into, but too small to draw it back out once its fist is clenched around the food. When the hunter approaches, the monkey goes into a panic. All it has to do is release the grasp of its hand, but it is too consumed by greed to do so.

In just such a way, the clenched fist of my obsession keeps me bound to Magee. All I have to do to free myself is to release my grasp on what is consuming me.

And I can't do it. I cannot.

So I wrote in my latest addition to my novel, in which truth was continuing to blend ever more inextricably with fiction. My good intentions at extracting myself from my madness had lasted all of twelve hours—until the next time I saw Magee.

What I really needed, I concluded, was to form a Magee Anonymous group: gather together all the men who had ever been obsessed with her, admit our powerlessness over the situation, and somehow begin the arduous task of overcoming it. I'd need to track down Fred Phillips, who had maintained her old Volkswagen, free of charge, during her entire tenure at Boscoe, keeping it not only in top running condition but continually filled up with gas. And Eddie Newbury, who'd spent a semester sleeping in the shrubbery outside her dorm, not wanting to miss a glimpse of her, until winter moved in and he nearly died of exposure. Then there was Bob Redson, who'd tracked her down several years ago after becoming a state senator, in hopes that he was finally worthy enough to marry her. Perhaps we could even admit Betty Greensward, who'd dedicated her three volumes of "coming out" memoirs to Magee. We were clearly going to have to rent a conference center, if not a sporting arena, for our meetings.

After that night alone with Magee, something had broken in me. Questions crowded my mind; confusion wrapped itself in smoggy layers around my thinking. Was Magee happy? Did she *really* love Max? Who *were* these people, anyway? The Buddhist texts I was reading said: anything you hold on to holds you back. But although I fought against it, I could feel myself slipping deeper. It was a dark, messy world that Max and Magee inhabited, and I was getting sucked into it, seemingly against my will. And try as I might, I couldn't raise the energy to extract myself.

I was certain she could know my thoughts. I became convinced that every comment, every glance in my direction, every time she placed a hand, however fleetingly, on my shoulder or arm, carried hidden meaning. She *must* be feeling the same way I was. It was simply inconceivable that such weight of emotion could be unreciprocated.

But then, isn't every compulsive, driven lover certain his love is reciprocated?

I was having it again: the feeling that something very bad was going to happen. And I wasn't going to be able to do a thing about it.

Max returned from New York all worked up about the new direction his writing was beginning to take. *The Telltale Breast* was due to come out any day, but he seemed much more excited about his next, as yet unwritten, project.

"Frankie, I'm in a bit of a . . . a . . ."—I watched him try to twirl the spaghetti of thought onto the fork of syntax, and fail—"a creative plethora right now." He was so pumped he could scarcely put his words in order; they just spewed in a torrent of verbiage. "I'm telling you, this next book is going to be my masterwork. I've got a couple of new titles, serious ones; check these out: *Toward Burgeoning Vistas.* What do you

think? Or maybe, *My Afternoon in the Morning.* This is a serious
project, Frankie, no more of this pulp stuff—it's a postmodern thing, a Dada-in-the-twenty-first-century thing, a symbolic interweaving of character and destiny—whaddaya think?
But truly, buddy, I'm ready to be taken seriously as a writer.
No, no"—he cut off my protests about the critics who praised
his work already—"I'm talking *really* seriously." When he got
like this his eyes went wide and his eyebrows writhed about
like drunken caterpillars and his arms spun like ship's propellers. His presence was so large he filled the room; there
was no space for anybody else. "How about *The History of Now?*
Or *Decade, My Decade . . . These Splintered Hills?*"

One thing his titles had going for them, I thought: *they were
consistent.*

Meanwhile, I was working feverishly on *The Finished Man.*
Coming up with *my* title that night with Magee had given me
a real shot in the arm. Every once in a while, though, I'd
stand in front of the mirror and look at myself. Still the same
old Frank. But who was I becoming? I wondered. Was I Finished? Would I ever be?

Max kept trying to reach his editor to talk about his new
ideas—but every time he answered the phone, thinking it
was a return call, it was his creditors instead. I'd hear him ar-
guing on the line in his office, then finally shouting "Fuck
off!" and slamming down the receiver.

"Do you know what that guy just said to me?" Max asked
after one of these conversations, steaming volcanically into
the living room and going straight to the liquor cabinet.

"Pay up or we'll take your house?" suggested Magee.

Max just coasted right by that one. "I asked him, 'How can you treat me this way? Don't you know who I *am*? I'm Max fucking Peterson.'

"And you know what he answered? 'But, Mr. Peterson, we treat *everyone* this way.' "

It was strange, though—no matter how much I heard Max talk about his new book, I never heard him working on it. The clatter of the Underwood, whose keys he attacked with such vigor that he'd worn off most of the letters printed on them, usually carried throughout the house. I knew, too, that he had a tight deadline. Maybe, I thought, that's why he spent so much of each day sleeping—he was up every night working. For all his excitement, he was keeping exceptionally closemouthed on the details.

I realized there was a lot I still needed to know about Max if I wanted to understand what made him tick. And I did. I needed to know the secret of his success—and not just in the literary arena.

I waited until the two of them had gone out for an afternoon and I was sure I'd have a couple of hours to myself. Then I slipped back into his study and started going through his papers. My actions may seem strange, but put yourself in my shoes. You feel compelled to understand this man. You feel compelled to sleep with his wife. . . . Have you ever found yourself living a life you never expected to live, doing things you never expected to do? That's how I felt. I'd already stepped over a certain line. Why stop there?

At least I'd struck upon a pretty good rationalization for my surreptitious activities—one that, ironically, I'd acquired from Max.

I was doing research for my novel.

I bypassed the top of his desk, after leafing briefly through it in search of anything that looked like a new manuscript—although this wasn't the object of today's search. This time, I wanted to dig deeper. My first discovery came from the lower left-hand drawer of his desk. It was a sort of writer's logbook, providing a unique tour through the author's mind. On the front page was penned an epigram that was, I thought, truly worthy of Max:

> *Every true artist must deal with all subjects. There is, finally, no "bad taste."*

On the next page I found the following list:

Possible Metaphors for the Moon
The moon hung in the sky like . . .
. . . a human skull
. . . a dog's water dish
. . . a saucer without a cup on it
. . . a very large aspirin tablet

> . . . *a bowling ball*
> . . . *a hubcap*
> . . . *a big puffy round white pillow*

Beneath that was a list headed **Story Ideas:**

> *Tell Satan's story from his side—maybe he wanted to go to*
>   *Hell because Heaven was so boring.*
> *A man discovers the perfect aphrodisiac—what happens?*
> *What if people came into heat, like animals do?*
> *A play about a hairdresser: My Hair Lady.*

Then came notes on writing and characters:

> *A noun is just a verb in a cage.*
> *Character idea: a man who masturbates to wind his self-*
>   *winding watch.*

Some bits were so strange I didn't know how to categorize them:

> *Sperm. That's what we're like. Millions of us, swimming up-*
> *ward in darkness, struggling toward some unimaginable*
> *goal. And for every hundred thousand only one makes*
> *it . . . to what? Success? Freedom? Redemption? Is this why*
> *we live—to fertilize God?*

> *Sometimes I feel like a baby chick that thinks he's got it all*
> *figured out because he knows the inside of his tiny eggshell*

universe. Then one day the whole thing cracks open, and
where do you find yourself? Under some hen's ass.

Interesting enough, but I knew there had to be more. I
felt like Philip Marlowe on a particularly challenging case as
I prowled through the rest of the drawers and a filing cabinet, pausing every so often to listen for signs of movement
in the house—and uncovering, incidentally, nothing that
looked like a new novel in the process. On impulse I shifted
my investigation to the bookcase. There, behind leather-
bound editions of Tolstoy, Dostoyevsky, and Dickens—none
of which appeared to have ever been opened—I found a hip
flask filled with Jack Daniel's, several packets of condoms,
and—bingo!—a thin bound volume with the words *Personal
Diary* in gilt letters on the front. The lock had been sprung
long ago, probably by Max himself, who couldn't hold on to
a key to save his life.

I sat down to examine the volume; to my disappointment, the entries all dated from our college years, a decade
ago. Still, I found myself fascinated by the glimpse it provided of Max in his formative period. His arrogance was
already firmly in place, as evidenced by the following sam-
pling:

*I feel like Sisyphus, and the rock is my own talent, which I must
roll painfully to the top of the hill, again and again. . . .*

*I don't want to play the game: to eat the shit of others so that
some day I can force them to eat mine. . . .*

I'm burning up, I'm hot all over, I'm in a fever to tell what I know: my circuits are overloaded, power filling me up like a current seeking a ground. To know that you are the one, to feel that knowledge burning inside you, to be on fire, filled with power and brilliance. . . . Nothing will stop me. I will move the world if I have to.

Poor Max, I thought. He would have made a good messiah, if only he'd been born in a better age for it. Certain entries exhibited an almost impassioned attraction for darkness:

If all life is a process of deterioration, then I want my decay to be beautiful. I want to go out like a comet, in a blinding, screaming flash of light.

I've often thought of suicide, not out of despair, but out of curiosity.

I seek union with the ugly, the perverse: I want to wallow in muck and filth, to breathe life's foulness, as I breathe its joy.

Then, too, there was a lyricism, an idealistic streak that I wouldn't have expected from Max—who, I was beginning to realize, qualified as one of the last great romantics:

A clear and bright and true idea rises, like the full moon, only once in a while; and there are many half truths and dark moonless nights between.

*We fall as snow; but most of us, by the end of our lives, have turned
to ice in the futile attempt to escape melting. We will melt, all and
all, one day.*

But where, I asked myself, was the real stuff? What would
Marlowe do in a situation like this?

O.K., I thought. *If I'm going to crack this case, I'm going to
have to think like Max.*

I went into his dressing room, selected a corduroy coat
from his closet and put it on, then draped one of his white
silk scarves around my neck. I examined myself in his mirror, turning this way and that. Not bad, but something
seemed to be missing. *Aha,* I thought. I found a box of his
mile-long cigars on his nightstand, stuck one in my mouth,
and lit it up to complete the effect. I sat there, looking at myself in the mirror. *So this,* I thought, *is what it feels like to be
Max.* I blew a billow of smoke out at the glass. *This is what it
feels like to have Magee.*

Then, as I stood there in his dressing room, all at once it
came to me. I don't know how to describe the chain of asso-
ciation I went through, except that it went something like:
secret life . . . underworld . . . underwear.

I found what I was looking for right there in the back of
his underwear drawer, beneath stacks of plaid boxers and
jock straps and "tightie whities," as we used to call them at
college. It was a standard notebook such as you might buy at
any bookstore, and I don't know why he had hidden it there
except that perhaps he figured there was no place in his

study where it would be safe from prying eyes—and he was right.

Heart rattling against my ribs, I opened the notebook and knew right away I'd hit pay dirt. It contained Max's hand-written notes—numbered, though scattered and sketchy—for what he'd called "his life's work." On the front page was written the title, in a bold calligraphic hand:

THE ONE HUNDRED FUNDAMENTAL VARIETIES OF WOMEN: A WORK IN PROGRESS

Below the title was an epigram:

There are no worlds left to conquer. Where is there to conquer, then, but in love?

Written in a kind of shorthand, many of the entries seemed quite peculiar—perhaps even fictionalized:

#37: Demoiselle de Des Moines: *Midwestern heart-of-the-earth girl, lips red as watermelon; strawberry blond hair coiffed into perfect curls. Wants me to hum the national anthem in the sack.*

#64: Soho Shrew: *Sharp-nosed sharp-eyed high-cheekboned woman from Manhattan with a tongue that could slice you into strips, fingernails bright red as though they'd been dipped in blood . . .*

"How much do you like me?" she asked.

"Not too much," I replied.

"That's good," she said. "That's the way I like it."

#58: Dreadlocked Damsel: *I couldn't have said if she was blond, brunette, or redhead. But I watched that hair and wondered what it was thinking. Her head was an octopus with a thousand arms. She told me, "Don't tangle with my mind"——but there it was, spilling down across her shoulders, and in clear need of a trim.*

#73: Woman of Extreme Amplitude: *I crawled atop her. She was enormous. I had to clear the flesh aside to find her opening. I felt myself sinking into her vast bulk; limp, flaccid, lumpy. . . . It was like quicksand. It was like pancake batter. I put my arm around her trackless waist, felt her interminable weight against me. . . . It was like making love to a mound of Jell-O. It was like making love to a mountain.*

So Max *had* been with Kitten Caboodle. This seemed the obvious conclusion to draw, considering this was the most recent entry. Still, what was it about these notes that bothered me? Was it the sense that Max was straining for effect? That there was a certain effort to convince?

I finally realized: it sounded as though he was writing for an audience, as though these scattered jottings were intended to be read. But if so, by whom? I drew at my cigar, and tapped the ash off in the sink. My head was starting to swim again. Could it be that Max, in his new desire to be taken seriously, was intentionally leaving tracks for some future scholar to follow? Attempting to create a final, ultimate fiction that would outlast him?

Then again, maybe it was me who was creating the fiction. Maybe Max was the sort of guy who was always onstage, even if the only audience was himself.

Still, there were other clues that his amorous adventures were perhaps not as universally satisfying as he'd like his public to believe. Consider **#72, Skid Row Siren:**

> *As her face hovered close to mine, poised for one last kiss, it blurred and split. Her eyes swam out of focus, separated and overlapped; it looked like there was an extra eye on her forehead. She smelled of old smoke and powder and stale perfume. She looked like a gorgon, a cyclops, as she fell back upon her pillow—a snoring Medusa. I lay beside her, turning to stone. I contemplated escape. I contemplated murder. And finally, I slipped over the edge, unknowing, into sleep.*

There were some blank pages, presumably intended for the twenty-seven conquests still awaiting his attention; then, on the last couple of sheets, a handful of ambiguous notes:

Henry: that weekend in Boston . . .

Might this be a reference, I wondered, to a visit to a brothel? Or someone his friend had set him up with back East?

Farther down the page was another ambiguous entry, presumably concerning some erotic adventure or other:

> *If I had strength I would have the power to stop this. How can it be that this is my fault, if I cannot find the strength to stop? And yet I feel I am somehow being held responsible. We've all been set up. God has framed us; we're taking the fall for Him. We're being held responsible for crimes we can't help committing.*
> *<u>This</u> is sin.*

Finally there was this closing entry:

> *Morality, immorality, virtue, honesty: these are the classifications of someone who has never really wrestled with them— like a scientist who can never understand what goes on beneath the sea, but must watch, baffled, from the surface, while another self he will never know cavorts and frolics, suffers and dies, in the depths below. . . .*

How crazy, I thought, yet somehow fitting. I was obsessed with *her* body—and *his* body of work. My private investigations had all added up to . . . what? By the time I was finished, I wasn't sure I understood Max—or Magee, for that matter—any better at all. If anything, I was only growing more confused.

At that moment I heard a sudden creaking sound from behind me. I sprang to my feet, cigar in hand, scarf swinging around my neck, to see the dressing room door slowly begin to open. A low, throaty sound, like a quiet growl, came from behind it. The door opened farther, then Vronsky stepped around the edge and into the room. He plunked himself down at my feet and immediately went to work cleaning his left paw. Then he paused and looked up at me with his head cocked to one side—grinning, I'd swear.

9

The Siege of Malomar

A SIMPLE bang on the head. That's how they did it in the movies. An unexpected fall down the stairs after having a few too many. A handful of sleeping pills in the Jack Daniel's. Make it look like an accident.

The question was no longer whether to do it. The only question was how.

And that question was growing more pressing by the day.

No, I wasn't intending to knock off Max. Though I must admit I'd been considering that fate for the character based on him in my novel—the plot of which was turning out to be considerably more lurid than my everyday life.

Fictions, see? It's all just fictions.

The idea had occurred to me, oddly enough, during meditation. Or should I say during one of my attempted meditations. After spending the last weeks in an unbearable state of tension, I was once again trying to take on a regular practice, in hopes it would bring equanimity, as all the texts said it would.

But no sooner did I sit down than the most dramatic picture show you ever saw started up in my head. Sex, mayhem, murder—you name it—the entire human condition played through my mind as I sat there on my little black cushion:

"You're the one I've always wanted. Ever since I first set eyes on you." She loosened the strap of her bra, revealing a smooth arc of collarbone above the soft curve of her breast. "And starting tonight, we're going to make up for lost time. . . ."

Predictably, the biggest blockbusters in the multiplex of my mind all featured the same leading lady. However, these scenes never went on long before her costar intruded, inspiring a sequence of scenarios I'd have preferred not to witness. Once Max appeared he tended to take over, tormenting me with scene upon scene of his liaisons with not only Magee but the other 73 Varieties I'd encountered in his journals: #69: Hot-Pants Housewife; #53: Motorcycle Maven; #64: Bestial Virgin. If these visions went on long enough, I might even find myself joining in.

Christ, I thought. I was becoming as bad as he was.

In Southern California the weather operates as though it's equipped with a switch: once it's thrown in a certain direction, it stays on until someone turns it off again. It wasn't long after Max's return from New York that whoever's in charge of such things flipped the device in the direction that read: *Rain*.

In the beginning the relief was palpable: the TV showed children playing in rain-streaked streets and lovers walking under umbrellas; experts analyzed the effect of the precipitation on the orange crop and whether it had been sufficient to reverse the drought. But by the time the torrent had been coming down for a week with no sign of abating, the verdict was clear: the switch had stuck in position.

"More, More, More!" Max proclaimed daily, looking at the glowering sky through our enormous front window when he finally got up around 2:00 P.M. For once it didn't seem to make a difference that he stayed up all night and slept into the afternoon; it was some version of dark all day long, and I imagined that this must be what life was like for people in the arctic, in the night that lasted all winter. Still, I couldn't help but wonder at the effect his increasingly nocturnal habits were having on his relations with Magee.

The sea threw itself against the cliffs and beachfront homes of Malomar; the wind wailed and screamed and moaned. Bits of the house flapped and banged. Asphalt shingles and pieces of tar paper—once I saw the entire tin roof of a shed—blew past the front window, whose surface buckled and flexed alarmingly against the onslaught. The rain came down in buckets and sinkfuls and washbasinfuls and finally by the bathtubful.

The Coast Highway to the north, just below Point Mojo,

slid shut under tons of mud, which sluiced down from hillsides stripped of vegetation by last summer's fires and
drought. After days of unsuccessful attempts to clear it, the
highway department threw up their hands at the endless
quagmire and closed the highway. The canyons were impassable too, filled with rock slides and mud.

Magee and I had reached an equivalent impasse in our relations. Things had been awkward ever since that night we
stayed up talking together; increasingly, we rubbed against
each other in an unspoken state of friction—although the
world was too damp at the moment for any of the sparks to
cause much damage. We had the house to ourselves every
morning and into the early hours of afternoon, when Max finally got up; but it seemed ever more difficult for us to be
natural around each other. Then again, maybe it was just that
I couldn't get natural around her, and the rest was my imagination. I couldn't tell anymore.

One day I came in from cleaning up some fallen branches
and leaf litter around the castle. I was hanging up my yellow
slicker when Magee walked into the hallway, looked at me
with her serious green eyes, and said, "We're trapped,
Frank."

I looked back at her. "I know."

Her eyebrows lifted in a quizzical expression. "What, did
you have the radio on up at the apartment or something?"

"Radio?" I said.

We stood there staring at each other in the hallway, the
steady drip drip of water falling from my slicker the only

sound. "I'm talking about the south highway sliding shut," she said finally. "What are *you* talking about?"

"Nothing," I said, stepping past her. "Nothing at all."

I could have stayed away, spent more time in my own quarters, I suppose, but I'd got in the habit of coming down in the morning for coffee and the habit just stuck. Besides, we all seemed to want company, for the world outside had begun to seem more than a little frightening: dark and glooming, with the hand of lightning reaching down to grab the land by the collar every so often and shake the thunder out of it.

I did go up to my apartment after that, and turned on the radio to hear the report. The southern stretch of the highway had been buried too, beneath a mud slide as deep and impassable as the one to the north. Magee was right. We were trapped.

For those who lived in Malomar, there was suddenly no way out.

The tempest outside was accompanied by the usual whirlwind of events inside: specifically, the ill-starred reception of Max's long-awaited second novel, *The Telltale Breast,* which had been released several weeks earlier. Despite Max's brilliant performance on the Cleverman show, the reviews were disappointing, to say the least.

Dead Prose Tells No Tales

read the headline in the "Holiday Gift Book Guide" section of the *Bronx Review*. And even Max's former champion August Snipe had panned the novel, titling his *LA Times* article:

Peterson Peters Out

"Second novel-itis," grumbled Max, moping about the castle and staring through the windows at the equally depressing scene outside. "Come out with a successful first novel, and the critics are gunning for you on the follow-up."

"Don't worry, Max," I reassured him. "This book is easily as good as *City of Breasts.*" This was no lie; I'd read it several weeks back and found it to be the undeniable equal of his first opus. "Your fans are bound to realize that."

"You know, brother," said Max—he'd lately taken to calling me "brother," a habit I found at once irritating and endearing. "I think you're right. Every author has setbacks. And then there's my new direction to consider. Just wait till *A Nascent Dawn* goes to press. . . ."

But near as I could tell, *A Nascent Dawn,* or *The Inverted Heart,* or whatever his next book was to be called, was going nowhere at all. When I asked Max about it, he claimed it was impossible to work with the weather so foul.

"An artist must never be false to himself." He tossed the tasseled end of his scarf over one shoulder with a flourish. "And working without inspiration is the height of falsitude."

"An artist must never be false to his *publisher,*" corrected

Magee. "*Or* his creditors. Or his wife. And there's no such word as falsitude."

The closed highway forced Max to cancel a series of readings scheduled to promote *The Telltale Breast*. Still, he stayed up all night and set off determinedly at 5:00 A.M. one morning in the Ocelot, in the blind certainty he'd be able to make his way out to Hollywood for an appearance on the *Wake Up USA* show. When he returned hours later, both he and the Ocelot had acquired a new full-body coat of mud. Without a word, he went to the liquor cabinet and poured himself a Jack Daniel's, though Magee and I were still sipping our morning coffee. Max had not only been unable to get out of Malomar by any conceivable route; the storm had shut down every telecommunications device in town, including his cell phone, and he hadn't even been able to call to explain his absence.

"There's no way out of this mudhole," he told us, gulping his bourbon like some mud-streaked 1950's movie gangster. "We're trapped like goddamned rats."

Despite Max's efforts to keep up his spirits, I could tell the situation was eating away at him. He played basketball by himself for hour upon hour, sometimes far into the night. Once I woke at 4:00 A.M. and, glimpsing an unusual glow coming in across my walls, peered out to find all the lights in the ballroom on. As I stood there I saw Max's silhouette rise against the window, poised for a jump shot, a cigar clenched between his jaws. He hung there, as though suspended in air, for a miraculously long moment before settling back to earth again.

I felt bad for Max, but I had to admit I felt a guilty throb of pleasure too. At least he couldn't have *everything* his way—the acclaim, and the house, *and* the wife—all the time.

But still the rains came down. The castle was so isolated, perched by itself up on that hillside, it made us all crazy. We had no neighbors. The restaurants and cafés nearby were mostly closed up. There was nowhere to go.

By the end of the first week I was going out of my mind with claustrophobia; between the sky, which the stage crew of heaven lowered closer to the ground every day, and the atmosphere, which felt entirely too damp and thick to breathe—particularly indoors, with the windows closed against the rain and wind, and the air thick with cigar and cigarette smoke. What I needed was air, and there didn't seem to be any of it in all of Southern California.

Finally things became so bad, between the storms and the mud, the record high tides and gale-driven waves that daily devoured more chunks of coastline—not to mention entire celebrity homes down at the Enclave—that they had to call in the military. Malomar became the most upscale disaster area ever declared by the U.S. government.

Magee was in a tremendous state of excitement. "They've brought in the Marines," she exulted. "Our heroes!" She shouted and waved from the driveway as helicopters filled with fatigue-clad stalwarts swooped like pterodactyls overhead on their way to the beachfront. Saving the Enclave, unsurprisingly, appeared to be their first priority.

"It's like having our own private apocalypse!" said Magee.

"Forty days and forty nights," nodded Max. "There's, let's

see—twenty-nine left to go. Do you think if we inflated the tires really full on the Trojan Hearse, Frankie, it might float? If we three survive we can interbreed after it's all over, start a new race."

Now, there was an idea I could live with—depending on who interbred with whom.

"Great for you guys," retorted Magee. "I'm the one'll have to do all the work."

"You call *that* work?" asked Max.

"I'm talking about suckling infants. Diapers."

"Oh," said Max. "Well, there won't be any diapers anymore. We'll have to use fig leaves. Or just dip their bottoms in the drink."

And so Malomar was cut off almost entirely from the outside world, which was, ironically, the way the residents of the Enclave had always wanted it.

Jesus couldn't get back to his family in East LA, and so he took my place in the garage apartment, while I moved back into the guest room in the turret. Lupe and Esperanza, on the other hand, couldn't get back into Malomar, so Magee, with the rather inept assistance of Max and myself, had to oversee everything around the house herself.

Max lumbered about the place in the red-checked outdoorsman's jacket that Magee called his "huntsman-save-my-child" coat, with one of his white scarves wrapped around his neck to stave off the dampness. Despite the slump in his career, he never tired of coming up with titles for his next book and trying them out on us: *This Passing Gift . . . Nobody's Waltzing . . . The Nose of the Sphinx.*

"'*The Nose of the Sphinx*'?" said Magee. "No, Max, that's terrible."

"Who are you to say what's terrible?" Max growled. "I know my own business."

"Yes, you know everyone else's business too, don't you?" she retorted.

Max just stood there and looked at her.

How Magee could know what was terrible anymore, after years of supporting Max in his projects, was beyond me.

Still, Magee didn't seem to be having any problems with inspiration. As our involuntary retreat continued to extend itself, I'd often come across her tucked away in some corner of the house, scribbling in her notebook—"working on my dreams," as she always put it, with an enigmatic smile.

When the wind and rain kept me awake I'd rise before dawn and watch from my turret windows as the light seeped back into the world, turning it from black to gray and then stopping, as though the earth had halted in its rotation. The days never grew brighter than that: the flat hue of slate, the dull gloss of brushed steel. The rain seemed to have washed all color from the universe. For once I was grateful for the immensity of our stucco fortress, our stronghold against the elements—although the rest of the world appeared to be turning into a moat around it.

"At least we're safe here," I said to Max and Magee over dinner one evening, as we watched the Marines tackle the crisis on the television screen.

"Sure," said Max. "As long as this slope holds."

And to judge by the TV reports, houses were slipping

down the hills left and right, as eagerly as kids on a play-ground slide. One or two went every day, sliding their effortless way down the destabilized hillsides as the ground turned to mush beneath them.

There was no bedrock, you see, in Malomar.

Then there was the phenomenon that became known to the world as the Malomar Rock. This was a truck-size boulder, poised to lose its grip on a dissolving hillside, several hundred feet above a cluster of seaside homes along the Coast Highway. These were fancy, flimsy-looking constructions perched on spidery legs above the ocean—upscale versions of those third-world huts-on-stilts that always appear on *National Geographic* programs. It was clear from the video footage that the Rock was not likely to have a positive effect if it landed on them. Experts debated nightly about how to deal with the new menace, while Max and Magee and I gathered around the TV—the two of them side by side on the sofa with the cats, me in the leather armchair by the fireplace.

"Detonation," one expert suggested, only to have someone point out the damage that would be caused by the fragments.

"Pick it up with a crane," hazarded another.

No way to drive machinery in on that disintegrating hillside.

"Helicopter?" the show's host put forth.

"Fasten it down with cables?" I said.

"Helium balloons?" suggested Max.

"Antigravity device?" ventured Magee.

I figured we weren't likely to solve the problem that night, so I went off to deal with the dishes. If I didn't do something, they'd still be there the next morning—if not the following week. Then I headed up to feed the dogs.

I came back to the living room just in time to see Magee handing Max a bulky sheaf of papers. It might have been a manuscript; I couldn't be sure, because Max slipped it immediately into a leather valise on the sofa beside him.

"That your new book, Max?" I asked.

"No," said Max. "Yes. Magee was just having a look over it. Little editorial stuff, you know? She's good at that sort of thing. Makes her feel involved."

He seemed to have intended this as a compliment, but Magee shot him a glance and they both went quiet.

"So, how's it coming along?" I asked.

"Fine, fine," Max said—a response that sounded a bit familiar, I thought.

We returned to watching TV—it was one of those reality programs, called *Disaster*—but then Max left to use the bathroom and I thought maybe I could get the straight story out of Magee. "So how does the new book look?" I asked.

She gazed at me for a moment, the bluish light from the screen playing across her features. "Actually," she said, "I think it may be the best thing he's ever written."

She must have seen my face darken, because she followed with: "What, didn't you think he had it in him?"

"Sure he's got it in him," I said. "Max is practically a god, isn't he?" With that I tossed the remote control on the coffee table and left the room.

Does everything have to come so effortlessly to him? I thought. *Does the guy always have to land on his feet?*

After the first week of the siege, we developed a new diversion: mounds of mud, like melting chocolate, began sluicing into our driveway, so that I, along with Jesus and Max—whenever he decided to get up—had to shovel away for hours every day, lest the morass rise up and engulf the castle. "The Unholy Trinity," Magee called us, bringing out trays of cookies and lemonade to lift our spirits, and shaking her head over our sludge-streaked forms, in mismatched slickers and boots, assembled from whatever rain gear was left in the closets after years of drought.

We made up work songs and sang them while the rain streamed down our faces. It ran off the end of my nose and chin, trickled down the back of my neck, worked its way into my jacket.

"I've been digging in the mudhole, all the livelong day . . ." Jesus turned out to have a fine natural tenor, and after we became bored with the few melodies we knew, he translated them for us one afternoon and we sang them in Spanish: *"Yo trabajo en el fango, por la entero día . . ."*

"Did I say love was the only adventure in the modern world?" said Max. "Make that love—and mud."

That afternoon, to my immense gratification, Jesus finally said, "Please, Mr. Peterson, I don't like it when you call me, 'Hey, Dr. Seuss.' "

Max, to his credit, apologized, and never did it again.

After the mud, it was time for the bath. The three of us were all immersed after our day's work, Jesus up in the apartment, me in the guest bath, and Max in his own tub, when all at once I heard a penetrating thud, followed by a crash that shook the house. My first thought was for Magee, who I'd last seen on the sofa, engrossed in her latest book. In a single motion I leapt from the tub, threw a towel around my waist, and hurtled downstairs, trailing water behind me. I found the living room empty; I sprinted down the kitchen hallway—or at least, came as close to sprinting as was possible wearing nothing but a towel—only to collide with Magee, who was headed back the other way. Her copy of *Their Eyes Were Watching God* was still in her hand, her finger tucked between the pages to hold her place.

"Are you O.K.?" I grabbed her by the arms, leaving moist handprints upon her sleeves. "What happened?"

Her green eyes were as wide as oceans. "There's a boulder," she said. "In our kitchen." She pointed over her shoulder to where, on a broken mound of tiles, surrounded by shattered glass, there sat a stone as big as a meteorite, looking as smug and out of place as one of those enormous fruits from a Magritte painting. It had apparently tumbled down the hillside, bounced off the driveway, and bounded right through the window.

At that moment footsteps sounded along the hallway. Magee and I leapt automatically apart. Max sauntered up, still tying the sash to his bathrobe. "Someone pass out or something?" He craned his neck to stare around us into the kitchen.

We were all standing there, gazing mutely upon the phenomenon, when a tentative tap sounded at the back door. I stepped past the rock and turned the knob to find Jesus, likewise clad in nothing but a towel. In our corner of Malomar this was becoming a genuine fashion trend. Jesus peered warily around the jamb.

"Everything O.K.?" he asked. "Mr. and Mrs. Peterson fighting again?"

After debating what to do, the four of us managed to roll the intruder out the back door and into the edge of the garden. Afterward, Magee brushed off her hands and looked at us, standing in our towels and robes in the moonlight.

"Three half-naked men," she said. "How'd I get so lucky?"

Still the situation continued to escalate. Wind and rain beat against the castle walls day and night, punctuated by the sounds of helicopters and sirens. With Esperanza and Lupe away, the place dissolved into chaos: dishes piled up everywhere; balls of cat fur mutated into new life forms in the corners. Then one day the electricity failed, and I learned something about Magee's relationship—or lack thereof—to the real world.

"Oh Frank," said Magee, truly distraught, "I really wish I could have a cup of tea."

Cup upon cup of Darjeeling was her daily regimen until sundown, at which point she generally switched over to wine.

"Well," I answered, "why don't you?"

"I can't," she mourned. "The power's out."

"So? The stove is gas."

"It's what?"

"It's a gas stove."

"So?" She stared at me.

"So, the burners run on gas." We stood there, at a conceptual impasse.

"But . . ." replied Magee, "isn't that still electricity?"

In the evenings we rediscovered, as Max put it, "The Lost Art of Conversation."

We talked—or tried to—about our first sexual experiences. I didn't have much to say on the subject. How could I tell them that my virginity, which I hadn't managed to lose until college, had been surrendered, in spirit at least, to Magee—although another body, now nearly forgotten, substituted for hers in the physical realm?

"I lost *mine* when I was fifteen," said Magee, launching into the subject with enthusiasm, "to a boy named John Edwards, who lived down the street. . . . That is . . ." She was beginning to sound uncertain. "That is, unless you count—"

"How about," cut in Max, "if we talk about the happiest people we've ever met, instead?"

One thing all of our examples had in common, I noticed: none of them were rich.

But my most uncomfortable moments came when Max and Magee prevailed upon me to read from my novel.

"C'mon, Frankie," Max urged. "That's why we're putting you up here in our private artists' colony, isn't it?"

"It's not ready," I protested. "It needs more editing."

"We don't mind if it's not perfect," Magee chirped, irritatingly.

"I'll read it to you both once it's finished, O.K.? I promise."

"Aw, c'mon," said Max. "It's the least you could do, seeing as how you don't have any real duties around here. . . ."

There it was, I thought, the story of my life: "He had no real duties."

Except for shoveling mud, that is—a responsibility that continued to deepen by the day.

The tides rose relentlessly higher, driven by waves and winds that howled before the gales. When low tide came it was lower than ever, as though the water was being sucked out to sea in a great inhale, before the next exhale that would huff and puff and blow all the houses down. We went for long walks on the mudflats, Alpha and Omega bounding ahead in tremendous, slobbering enthusiasm, picking up dead stingrays and bits of unidentifiable carcasses and dropping them at our feet.

There were miles of flats, strewn with flotsam and jetsam—"Sea wrack and sea ruin," as Magee termed it: coils of kelp, brown and green, with ridged leaves like the fins of undiscovered sea creatures, their stems fleshy cylinders of green, twelve feet long, hollow and broken open; dead fish by the dozens, the hundreds; shattered fragments of shells, brilliant and gleaming; lost fishing buoys. There were timbers from ships, covered in pitch and barnacles, and huge pilings torn from ruined piers; shattered pieces of wood and glass that might have come—though I hoped not—from the hidden alcove. There was even an entire wooden dinghy, torn from its moorings and cast ashore as though in warning, one side smashed in, keel pointing upward as though it had rolled over before expiring. Clouds of flies rose from anything that had once been living if you nudged it with your foot, as though its soul was rising before your eyes.

My life was like this, I thought—storm-tossed and tumbled; chaotic, random; swept out to sea and thrown back in again, covered in dead fish and swarming with flies.

Once, during a break in the weather, Magee and I walked far to the north on the flats, past headlands you usually couldn't get around. But when the tide turned it turned on a dime, and we had to run back around outcrops of black rock, knife-edged with barnacles, through water that crested up onto our thighs—no way out except through, no way up those sheer-walled cliffs. The dogs were strong swimmers, bounding and tumbling their way over the surf; but the only way Magee and I could stay upright amidst the tumult was by holding hands and pulling each other along. When at last we were safe on shore, the sun broke through and for a moment—an almost golden moment—I felt like everything was all right between us again.

For a time it was quite an interesting adventure—like being Boy Scouts on a permanent picnic. But after a couple of weeks the fun began to wear off—especially after Jesus took advantage of a momentary opening in the southbound lanes to get home to his family, saying he'd be back as soon as he could. But since the return lanes were at the base of the cliffs, directly in the path of the oncoming slides, we knew we wouldn't be seeing him any time in the foreseeable future. After that it was Max and me and the muck, shoveling every day by ourselves.

"Even Jesus has forsaken us!" Magee couldn't resist saying.

I didn't bother moving back into my apartment at that point. What was I going to do, slog back and forth through the quagmire five times a day? Besides, we were all in this together.

When the power failed we listened to the boom box: Max's favorite bands, the Splash and the Clit Rifles.

"Decadence," Max crowed into the darkness. "I like decadence!"

Sometimes Magee put on her old Bobby Zipperman tapes, particularly the classic *Mud on Their Backs,* her favorite. Until the batteries ran out; then we sat in silence, Max and Magee smoking in the dark till there were no more cigarettes, at which point Max deferred and let Magee work her way through the remaining butts in the ashtray while he switched over to Swizzle Sweet cigars, raspberry-flavored—the only brand we'd been able to find left in all of Malomar. "Cigars for three-year olds!" he groused.

This marked the beginning of the *real* crisis.

After Magee exhausted the ashtrays in the house, she had to begin fishing through last week's trash for still-useable butts. The bags were piled high in the laundry room, since the garbage trucks had been absent for over a week. The Enclave Market and the few other open shops had run out of cigarettes days ago, and the last, desperate supply I'd procured for Magee by running down to the store on foot had been, to her disgust, a carton of ultralight menthols. She'd had to tear the filters off to get any actual smoke out of them.

We ran out of candles. We ran out of Jack Daniel's. Max was reduced to drinking peppermint schnapps—of which, for some reason, there seemed an unending supply in the liquor cabinet—first mixed with Coke, then with Perrier, then finally straight up. It only made him more manic than ever. Magee played Chopin on the piano: long, languid pieces in the pitch darkness. We bumped into each other in hallways, clutching at accidental flesh, always thinking whoever we touched was someone else.

The remaining food in the refrigerator went bad. The freezer defrosted itself, and the Enclave Market had run out of anything anyone would actually want to eat. My final purchase had yielded a jar of capers, a tub of Crisco, and a box of Bisquick. After several days munching our way through defrosting TV dinners, we'd started in on whatever canned goods were left in the pantry—mostly creamed corn and baked beans, neither of which I can eat to this day. At last we found ourselves sitting around a pathetic trayful of soggy biscuits Magee and I had concocted by combining the Crisco, Bisquick, and capers.

"All we need now," said Max, chomping tragically at a mouthful of paste, "is an earthquake."

"These wouldn't be so bad"—I pried my tongue loose from the roof of my mouth—"if we had some tuna or something to go on them. I could've sworn there were a couple of cans left on the top shelf in the pantry, but—"

"I fed them to the cats," said Magee.

We both turned to stare at her.

"You fed the *tuna* to the cats?" Max's eyebrows arched skyward.

"They were out of food."

"You could've fed them dog kibble."

"But they don't like it."

"You think *I* like these biscuits?"

Luckily, we were well stocked on kibble; the garage was stacked with bags that Max and Magee had delivered every week by a high-end Malomar pet service. We figured if we really got in a pinch we could always eat it, then move on to the dogs and cats. After that, Magee and I decided, we'd eat Max.

"We'll have to, darling," said Magee over his protests. "You've got more meat on your bones than any of us."

But Max had lost his sense of humor entirely, and we couldn't get so much as a chuckle out of him.

"I know," said Magee suddenly. "Let's call out for a pizza."

"Bright idea," responded Max. "What makes you think they're going to be open?"

"Maybe they have gas stoves," shrugged Magee, with a hint of a smile. "And the phone lines are working again, so it can't hurt to call."

Remarkably, they were open, working by candlelight at their gas stoves just as Magee had predicted, and providing sustenance to much of Malomar. Max, who was openly salivating by this point, voted for pepperoni, while Magee and I wanted bell peppers and olives. "Get them both," said Max. "Get them all. Just get them!"

But our preferences proved entirely theoretical when I got the owner on the line. "We're down to tomato paste and Velveeta," he said. "I'm afraid that's all we've got left."

Although we couldn't get a car down the mud-ridden

driveway and through the jammed electric gate, Magee miraculously managed to get our cabbie on the phone. He agreed to drive up with the pizza and meet us at the foot of the driveway. We were ravenous after shoveling mud all day—even Magee had pitched in for an hour or two.

For my money (Max's, actually), it was just about the best pizza I ever ate.

During low tide, on walks past the Enclave, I saw celebrities out sandbagging their houses—doing it themselves, as there was no one left to hire and there weren't enough Marines to go around. Sometimes I'd just find them wandering the beach in a daze. I saw Pirouette Wilson and Sandy Giblet and once I thought I caught a glimpse of old Bobby Zipperman, but it was just a lost, stoned surfer. They'd start sandbagging ever more frantically as the tide began to turn, and I'd hurry to help them as the sea came back up, its mouth wide open, eating away the mudflats in ferocious gulps, the spray already breaking over their decks as we put fresh boards over the seafront windows to replace those that had been stripped away by the tide before. I don't know where these people went after that, for the motels were already full of the stranded and dispossessed; somehow I always pictured them huddled inside while the waves flung themselves against the barricaded windows and poured in beneath doors, seeping across carpets, rising in wet circles along the legs of chairs, groping at electrical cords, swallowing VCRs, stereos, home entertainment systems—for who can keep out the sea? We came from her, af-ter all—as Magee had grown fond of saying—and now she seemed to determined to take us back.

When the tide went out it seemed I could feel it pulling inside me too, as though the water inside was trying to get back to the water out there. It felt as though I was being drawn out to sea against my will—but then, I guess I'd felt that way ever since I came to Malomar.

Every once in a while the clouds would part and I'd see the outline of lonely, battered Catatonia Island on the hori-zon and wonder how the poor souls out there were faring. I thought about the hidden alcove too, and how it was holding up, wherever it was—what a place that would be, I thought, to watch the spectacle of the storm.

In the third week the castle started leaking. We put out buckets, basins, paint cans—anything we could find, up and down the hallways, so that we were always tripping over them, sloshing water about, having to clean it up. We placed drop cloths over the piano and electrical equipment, poked into rooms I'd never seen before—many of which turned out to be empty, as there was far too much space in that house for Max and Magee to actually use.

"It's like the fall of Western Civilization," said Magee, looking upon the chaos.

It got so cold on nights the power was out—for although the furnace was gas, the thermostat and fan were electric—that after we'd run through the small supply of firewood Max had in for the winter, we were at a loss for what to do.

"I know," said Max, staring out the window in his plaid

jacket, scarf wrapped around his neck. "We'll burn the fence."

"The fence?" I said.

Max and I started pulling down the broad planks of the wooden fence that fronted the downhill side of the property, a few boards every day. We dried them in the corners of the living room, then split them up and burned them in the enormous stone fireplace. We'd demolished two-thirds of it before the electricity became reliable again, and it never did get rebuilt for all the time I lived at Malomar.

Every time we switched on the TV—when it was working—it seemed there were more and more preachers:

"Your trust in Jesus is your charge account in the Department Store of Deliverance. Choose from its many useful items . . . a Waring twelve-speed blender! A new Westinghouse microwave! . . ."

Families who had been washed—or slid—out of their homes were sleeping in the gymnasium over at Saltspray, while helicopters flew in supplies. Although we were almost out of food ourselves, we did carry loads of extra blankets and pillows and clothes down to the Enclave Market to give to the relief teams. We didn't see the sun or moon—either of God's two eyes—for days at a time.

Malomar was becoming more like the real world by the moment.

One day I was in the house by myself—Max and Magee had taken advantage of a lull to run the dogs, who'd been going crazy being locked up—when the phone rang. I should've just let it go; after all, chances were it was one of Max's creditors. But without thinking I picked it up.

"Hello?" I said.

"Who are you?" said a man's voice on the other end—an East Coast accent, harsh and suspicious.

"Who are *you*?" I came back.

"A friend of Max's." Silence hung on the line.

"I'm Frank," I said. "Their lodger."

"I didn't know Max had a lodger." Silence again.

"He does. They do."

"Well, hey, tell him Henry called, wouldja? Tell him . . . Henry's got something for him."

"O.K.," I said, not knowing how to take this.

"Oh, and—hey, as long as it was you who answered the phone, don't say anything to his wife, all right?"

"O.K.," I said, and hung up.

Something just didn't feel right about the whole exchange. I never did give Max that message.

Something occurred to me after all this had been going on for a while. Given all the people who had come to the parties over the summer, and considering that everyone in the region knew what was going on in Malomar, it was funny that nobody—aside from my mother and Aunt Clara—had phoned to check that we were all right. In fact, aside from the creditors, a couple of business calls, and that one from Henry, no one had phoned at all. I suddenly realized: beneath all the glamour and glitter, I was Max and Magee's only real friend.

One of the last nights before the rain stopped, I had a dream. The sea was rising up our driveway, lapping at the doors of the castle, until it began to pour in. We tried to find a way out, but there was no escape. At last the water began coming up over my head. As I sank beneath it I fought to hold my breath, but I finally had to let go and inhale—only to find, to my amazement, that I could breathe just fine.

That afternoon Max came back exultant after a walk on the beach with the dogs.

"I've got it!" he announced, blowing into the living room with all the force of the gale behind him.

"Got what?" said Magee and I in unison.

"The title for my next book. The serious one. I'm going to call it *Oysters in the Storm.*"

Strange as it sounds, in the final days of the siege of Malomar, the thermostat went wild, perhaps from the constant on-again off-again of the power, and there was no way to turn the furnace back down. We sat there baking, unable to control the heat, the three of us, stuck in the house, burning up together.

10

On Fire

ALL HUMAN beings recognize the simple perfection of the crescent moon, hanging low in a twilit sky, like a curved crack in the surface through which one may glimpse other worlds. Or the full moon, standing against the firmament like a hole punched out of a stage curtain, spilling in light from the other side.

But there is something about the three-quarter moon, with its one crisp edge and its one fuzzy edge, its lopsided neither-here-nor-there shape like a deflating football—so that it looks as though, were it not fastened into position, it would surely topple over—there is something about this moon that always fills me with discomfort and foreboding.

Now was the time of the three-quarter moon, and as I stood on the patio in the evenings watching it, that's the way my entire life felt: awkward, out of balance, and about to tip over.

So I wrote in my manuscript, and so I felt.

We were experiencing a brief, gorgeous spring, provoked by the rains, which would not come again for another
six months. Butterflies, birds, flowers, bees—the whole
nine yards. The air was dense with the scent of honeysuckle
and rose; the bougainvillea rose up to engulf the walls of our
castle in bright pink and purple exclamation points. Max
was away, seeing magazine editors and publicity people
about *Oysters in the Storm*—the manuscript of which,
through some miracle, he'd managed to deliver, and which
they were now rushing into production for summer.

At least, that's what he told us—I thought it possible he
was on another type of tour entirely.

It's funny, but ever since I'd moved in at Malomar, Max
had become secretive, and rarely confided in me as in the
old days. Maybe it was that I'd become too close, particularly after the claustrophobia of the siege, and he thought I
might let his secrets slip to Magee. I'd noticed him engaged
in surreptitious phone conversations more than once, however, and was relieved not to be involved in his deceptions.
Several times I answered their phone when I was in the
house, only to hear the click on the other end that told me I
was not the intended recipient of the call.

I was trying to devote myself to my writing; and at last it
seemed I was making real progress. But my renewed inspiration had its cost: I was thinking about Magee so much I was
making myself physically sick. Whatever I ate went straight
through me. I spent long, agonized hours perched atop the

porcelain bowl of my torment, thinking only of Magee. Yes, it bothered me, too, that I was pondering my one ideal of love and beauty while beset with intestinal cramps, but there was little I could do about it. I thought about her all the time, the same way she smoked cigarettes—one thought after another; and I could not quit.

I'd gone off to Newark for a month over the holidays, and when I'd returned things seemed to have settled down—it continued to rain off and on, but not enough to provoke another disaster, just enough to provide the land with its usual rainy-season nourishment. I'd found Max and Magee working steadily, both of them vanishing into Max's study for hours at a time—though I rarely heard the sound of the typewriter until the week before the book was due, at which point it started up around the clock, filling the house with its pounding clatter. Not having seen Max in a deadline situation before—*The Telltale Breast* was already complete when I came on the scene—I assumed this was the norm: last-minute, panicked activity, and Magee helping him, I supposed, with revision, proofreading, and the like.

I'd made a visit to my father while I was back East—the first such encounter in more than a year—and found him in poor form, physically at least: bedridden and unable to speak. Although he was responsive enough, gesturing when something of interest took place on the television, and nodding or shaking his head in answer to simple questions, he was unable to give any clear evidence he even knew who I was. Still, he seemed oddly content, even cheerful with his lot. And why not, I thought—all his needs were taken care of; he was even changed, several times a day, like an enormous infant—he didn't have to worry about a thing.

My mother and Uncle Charlie were the same as ever, full of questions about how soon I was going to finish my novel and suggestions about my future plans. Mostly, however—and most annoyingly—they wanted to hear about Max. My uncle Charlie had read both *City of Breasts* and *The Telltale Breast* since returning home and was convinced that Max was the most important new voice in American fiction since Hemingway.

Both of them persisted in calling me Frankie.

"Are we not drawn onward, we few, drawn onward to new era?" palindromed Uncle Charlie in parting, having reminded me that the door to the vast world of the dry-cleaning industry was always open to me.

I thought, but did not reply: *No, sir, prefer prison.*

And so a certain somberness had settled on my mood, which I tried to channel into my work, not knowing what else to do with it.

Malomar was known for its temperate climate as compared to the rest of the city, with its cool breezes coming off the ocean. But by May the air already seemed unnaturally still, and my garage apartment, which I'd moved back into after the siege, was sweltering. The abundant rains had caused an overgrowth of ground cover, and experts were warning of one of the most dangerous fire seasons in history. I'd been trying to stay away from Magee, hoping abstinence would *not* make my heart grow fonder. It would certainly improve my digestion, I thought, and my passions might find a healthier and more reliable outlet through my novel—which, consequently, was becoming awfully heated up, and even a little torrid. But between Max being out of town and our equidistant position between the seasons of rain and fire, life in Malomar, for once, was relatively calm.

That is, until the Sunday afternoon Magee burned the phone. She told me the beginnings of the event later—I was down walking on the beach at the time—but I saw the end results for myself. Ever since Magee caught on to the principle of the gas stove, she'd reveled in tea-making, acquiring all sorts of new gadgets: strainers and pots, bowls and whisks for green tea. She liked ritual, I'd come to realize, and between making tea and smoking she always had something to do, at any hour of any day.

She'd been in the kitchen, she told me, talking to Max on the phone. It was the first time he'd called in a week, and by her account the exchange was a bit testy. Meanwhile, she was making the preparations for a pot of Darjeeling. Max and Magee hadn't ever gone cordless, or even digital with their communications systems. Magee had an old-fashioned rotary phone she treasured, that she'd found in a flea market somewhere, of a peculiar purplish color she insisted on calling lavender. I don't know how she'd managed to find a lavender dial phone; I'd certainly never seen one before, and for all I knew it was the only such model in existence. But I'd have to say it suited her. She liked to have the twirly receiver line to play with while she talked, twisting it around one finger and then the other, in between lighting cigarettes, making tea, re-arranging the spices in the cabinets and such. For someone who often didn't seem like she did very much, she could be a flurry of activity when talking on the phone. She'd purchased an extra-long cord so she could walk around while she talked, holding the main part of the device beneath one arm, receiver crooked between shoulder and ear. That afternoon, she told me, after she and Max hung up she set the phone down, turned on the burner beneath the kettle, and went into the living room to retrieve her favorite mug.

Magee was standing beside the front window when she smelled, and then saw, a dark thread of smoke snaking along the hall, just below the ceiling, from the direction of the kitchen. Her first thought was for the phone—partly because of her attachment to it, but also because she needed to call the fire department. There were other phones in the house of course; but whether because of a protective impulse toward that one, or on pure instinct, she'd sprinted down the hall to get it.

Magee rounded the kitchen doorway just in time to see her lavender phone burst into flames. It sounds like an odd thing to happen, but as she explained it, she must have set it down with the cord too close to the burner, and the old-style plastic lit up like a fuse and carried the flame back to the phone. She caught one glimpse of it igniting, before a black wave of smoke came up and covered everything.

Instinctively she kept moving, out the back door and into the driveway. Then she realized she still needed to call the fire department. She ran around to the front door, but found it locked; she searched her pockets and discovered she'd left her keys inside. The kitchen by now was full of smoke, so she couldn't go back that way. Jesus and Lupe and Esperanza all had Sunday off, and I was down at the beach.

"The only phone I could have reached was *my* phone," she told me later, "—and it was the phone that was on fire. Isn't that just like me? So I was standing there watching the smoke pour out the kitchen door, thinking, *if I don't do something the whole place is going to burn down.* I looked around in desperation, and my eye fell on that straw doormat by the back door—and right next to it I saw the water spigot coming out of the wall. All of a sudden, I got this insane idea. I know I shouldn't have done this, but the nearest house was five minutes away and by the time I'd gotten down the driveway for help it would have been too late.

"I turned on the spigot and soaked the doormat, and sprayed some water over my head and my clothes, and I found an old rag lying around and soaked it too. And then—I know this is crazy, but I crawled back into the kitchen on my belly, holding the rag to my face and dragging the wet doormat behind me. I tried to stay below the smoke, holding my breath as much as I could, moving along by feel until I was just below the stove. Then, holding on to one corner of the doormat, I flung it up onto the top of the burner where the phone was. There were all these terrifying sizzling and popping sounds, mixed in with the wailing of the teakettle —then I yanked back on the doormat and the phone fell to the floor, and I got out of there as fast as I could, dragging the whole mess behind me. By that time I was coughing and choking and my eyes were tearing up so I couldn't see. . . . I collapsed on a rock and just sat there watching the phone sizzle and trying to catch my breath until you came back."

The first thing *I'd* heard when I was halfway up the drive was the teakettle howling through the open door, though at first I couldn't tell what the sound was—then I looked up and saw the black smoke and steam rising, and I started running. I burst around the curve at the top of the driveway to find Magee, soaked through and covered in soot, crying in front of a smoldering mound that I eventually identified as the telephone-plus-doormat. The kitchen door was standing open and smoke was still pouring out. But all I could think about was Magee. She heard my footsteps and rose and turned at the same time. The next thing I knew she was in my arms . . . again.

I held her for a long time until she'd calmed down, my own heart beating against my rib cage like a trapped bird. I could feel her breath coming first in quick gasps, then gradually slowing. At last she stepped away, leaving the wet imprint of her body against my T-shirt. Her hair was in a tangle around her face, and between the drops that fell from it and the ones still falling from her eyes, her skin was patterned into a sooty chaos of streaks and teardrop shapes. Never, I thought, had she looked so beautiful.

After I managed to confirm that Magee was all right and she didn't think the phone had caught anything else on fire, I made my way into the kitchen. The smoke from the smoldering plastic stung my nose and lungs; I pictured a lavender-colored residue lining my airways. I switched off the burner under the kettle, which was about to boil itself dry and start a second blaze. Strange, I thought, how it had continued to sit there doing its job, oblivious to the rest of the crisis, although its shiny copper body was completely blackened.

Then I phoned the fire department from Max's office to come check out the situation, just in case. I opened as many windows as I could—the rest of the house seemed fine, although the fumes had spread throughout the first floor at least, and the walls and ceilings from the hallway back to the kitchen were dark with soot. I searched for Leon and Vronsky, but they must have exited through the cat doors when the excitement started. Then I got my old siege-era rain slicker from the front closet for Magee to throw over herself, and brought her out a packet of cigarettes.

"You're right," said the fire chief, after determining to his satisfaction that the blaze was out. "The whole thing would've gone up—those curtains and the wood cabinets, and then it would've been into the ceiling and the beams. But still, you shouldn't have gone back in there. You're lucky to be alive."

In my big yellow slicker, her face smeared with soot, standing out in the driveway smoking a cigarette, Magee looked a bit like a fireman herself.

"Next time my phone burns," she told him, "I'll be more careful."

The chief pulled the doormat aside with his foot to inspect the blackened purplish mass with all its innards spilling out on the driveway.

"My beautiful phone!" mourned Magee.

We retreated to my garage apartment——the atmosphere in the house was still too choking and poisonous to want to be in there, and Magee refused to go inside at all.

"You have a nice place here." Magee sat with a cup of tea, light playing across her face as she looked out through my rectangular cutouts of sea and sky. "So simple and relaxing. I may never go back."

I went down and collected provisions for the evening: snacks and a bottle of wine, another packet of cigarettes. I made sure the cats and dogs had enough food and water. And lastly, at her request——what filmy, lovely, beautiful things I found there!——I went through Magee's dresser to find her a change of clothing. In the last drawer, I found something I probably wasn't supposed to see. There, beneath a pile of lacy underthings——silken-smooth camisoles and tights, nylons and chiffons, satiny cups and straps, gauzy nets and meshes, pleats and gathers, hooks and wide-open eyes—— there I discovered, tucked into the back corner, a pile of handwritten pages, an inch or more thick, in a plain manila folder.

So Magee had a manuscript too.

It took an act of will, I must admit, to disengage my attention from her undergarments. But once I'd succeeded, I couldn't resist slipping out a random page to have a look. It read:

> *Do you know how much I love you?*
> *I love you as much as all the salt in all the oceans, as much*

as all the sand in all the deserts, as much as every ant in every anthill, every blade of grass on every suburban lawn. I love you as much as every cloud in every sky, every snowflake that has ever fallen. . . .

I love you as much as every sneeze that's ever been sneezed, every french fry that's ever been fried, all the teeth that have ever been collected by the tooth fairy. As much as every bit of stardust swept from the stars every morning—which is why they shut them down during the day, so they can be all new and clean and polished for the night to come.

Ah, I reflected, all the bright fishes of Magee's imagination, shimmering in schools of thought! What a marvelous thing. Though I might not, admittedly, have been the most unbiased observer.

Still, I felt a pang of jealousy run through me. Who could she possibly love *that* much? Surely not Max.

O.K., Frank. I had to tell myself. *It's just fiction.*

I felt peculiar standing there with her words in my hand: a sense of guilt rummaged about my interior—which seemed strange, considering the fact that rummaging through her lingerie hadn't bothered me in the least.

But Magee was waiting for her clothes, and in any case, I couldn't bear to be away from her for long. I slipped the manuscript back into place, then went up to the apartment. While Magee showered and changed I called our cabbie on my phone. He brought us up a pizza for dinner, provoking a whole new round of stories and explanations about the afternoon's events. Then Magee and I sat up in my apartment, picnicking on pizza and wine, and watching the last of the colors change over the water.

After that—I don't know, but it just felt natural, and fitting, and proper, that Magee should slip into my arms again.

We stayed together in my apartment for the next week, while teams of workmen arrived to repaint the kitchen and hallway and replace the tile and cabinets and do whatever it was they had to do to get the smell out of the house—though they never could erase the blackened, perfect imprint of the coiled receiver cord that started it off the stovetop; and Magee, who liked design, refused to have the unit replaced.

Jesus, Lupe, and Esperanza all turned a blind eye—or else they believed our story that Magee was forced to sleep on my couch because the lingering smell in the house brought back the horrors of the fire. But it did seem that I saw a new glint in Jesus's glance; and the trace of a smile crossed his lips whenever, in passing, he greeted me.

And perhaps it ought to have been obvious to the workmen—or someone—that we rarely left the apartment, except for an hour or two before sunset every day, to walk together on the beach, in that brief but seemingly infinite succession of glorious, golden afternoons.

It was as though all the friction of the past months had begun to produce sparks, that ignited us at last.

But then the work was finished and the workmen went away. And Max came home, and I had to give her back.

II

The Big Heat

PASS, TIME, oh sweet time, and bring me to my lover!
Never have I so hated time, and yet so loved it. Hated it for
keeping Magee from me; loved it for being the vehicle that
would bring her back again.

And hated it more once we were together——for even in
the first passionate moments of our meetings, when hours of
love still lay ahead, I felt time preparing to take her from me
once more. . . .

Truth was becoming less and less distinguishable from
fiction.

The fiction was still going well, in the realm of my novel,
at least. But winning the woman of your dreams, I was beginning to realize, was only another form of torture, unless
she became completely yours in the process.

We limped along, Magee and I, grabbing moments here and there when Max wasn't watching; risking quick, uneasy visits to my apartment in the mornings while he slept; occasionally spending an entire evening together when he was off somewhere. The relationship took on that curious intensity that only comes when there is no future or thought of future. And even the nebulous present was doomed to end, and I couldn't bear to think of it.

I had the keys to the kingdom—but, like the family car, only when Dad wasn't using it.

I kept wondering about Magee's manuscript—and who this mysterious "you" was that the narrator loved so much. Once, I admit, I even looked for it again, hoping to read further, but she must have thought better of her hiding place and moved it elsewhere. And I could find no way of bringing up the subject that wouldn't arouse her suspicions.

I walked the beach endlessly, searching for the hidden alcove, our perfect refuge; but I never could find it.

Needless to say—for God, fickle and whimsical creature that He is, smiles without discrimination on whoever He wants to—*Oysters in the Storm* became the biggest hit of Max's career, despite what Magee and I thought was his most ridiculous title yet. It shot to the top of the best-seller list within a few days of its release and remained there for week upon relentless week.

The cover to the *Cuyahoga Quarterly* featured a grinning Max, cigar in hand, above the headline:

Peterson Weathers the Storm

The *New Brunswick Star* exulted:

The World Is His Oyster

August Snipe, in a complete roundabout, praised Max's "muscular and prophetic new voice" and proclaimed him the "most compelling writer in America."

Paranoid Studios, who owned the option on the book, hired Max to write the screenplay. His renewed success had provided him with a fresh burst of creative energy, and following an intensive reading tour, Max settled into a fury of night-long cutting and revising, trying to fashion the thing into a script. Perhaps equally needless to say, he failed. Still, after a succession of rewrite men had clambered onto the apparently sinking ship, it bobbed again to the surface, and the Muscular, Prophetic Masterpiece was rushed into production. To Magee's chagrin, the ethereal Guinevere Pilchard—the cloud-woman from the Friday the 13th party—had been cast as the heroine.

"Is she on your list?" I asked Max.

"Who's that?"

"Guinevere Pilchard."

He didn't answer.

The money, when it came through, was going to be enough to bail him out of debt—not to mention, as he put it, "doing a few little improvements around the place."

"And, hey—maybe we'll even finally get you some curtains for that apartment," he added. "Huh, brother?"

I had to shake my head in wonder. His life was ashes, but Max rose from it again and again.

He'd just received, and was in the process of having Jesus install in the garden, another gift from his publisher: a stone angel, peeing. "This is going to look great next to the Venus de Milo," he said. "What do you think?"

"Great, Max," I said. "I can hardly wait to see them squirting away side by side."

I stood back and looked at the figures. For the first time it struck me that the Venus, a perfect replica of the original de Milo, had no arms. All she could do was stand there and look beautiful. She couldn't actually *do* anything.

Max came and went through the early part of that summer. When he was home, my waiting for another moment with Magee was agony. When he left, I was near ecstasy. Each minute with her seemed infinitely precious; each second was a piece of glass that, if dropped by the hand of awareness, might break.

I felt like life had become an elaborate game of chess in which I, the pawn, had to respond continually to the unpredictable moves of the king and queen.

But how to communicate what it was like in those moments we *were* together? We rolled in the mountains in fields of poppy and lupine, tumbled in secluded coves at Point Doom. On days the fog never lifted, we drove up to the top of Mulehauler Drive, until we came out above the cloud layer in the bright, impossible sunlight, shining up there all on its own, the clouds stretching out to the horizon beneath our feet like a fluffy white carpet, so firm it seemed we could walk on it, and no one there to see it but us.

For we had to hide not only from Max, but from Lupe, Esperanza, and Jesus as well.

Hiding from Jesus, we laughed!

But the greater landscape was the landscape of Magee, which I came to know so intimately—the slope from her lips down to the slight cleft of her chin, the long glide of my tongue over the swoop of her throat . . . across the tucks and dips of her neckline; the taut ridges of collarbones lifting beneath the skin as though wanting to free themselves—the curve of flesh that rose to her breasts, and from there along the faint, moist arroyo at the midline of stomach that rose and fell with her breath, along the cleft of navel to the hollow of hipline, until before me rose the treasure I'd dreamed of for over a decade. . . .

The scent of her overwhelmed me: like apples and like grass; like flint struck against stone; like roses. She could never move through a room without leaving her mark on the very air. Why should it be that I found the unseen, un-visible part of her so compelling? Worlds rose and died in the faint traces of scent along her thighs and the insides of her elbows. . . . Other men had their New Worlds, their Antarcticas and Northwest Passages, their East Indies and Everests, but for me it was always and only and forever Magee.

I was beside myself. "Look at your beautiful shoulders," I

cried. "Look at your beautiful neck. Look at your beautiful collarbones!"

"Frank, you're getting boring," Magee laughed, now that our simmer had come to a boil and the pot boiled over. . . .

Then she'd look in the mirror, turn this way and that, and ask: "Frank, what is the most wonderful thing about me?"

Now I had to laugh. "Your ears—shapes of sheer perfection, classic in their proportions—"

"Which is more beautiful," she persisted, "my eyes or my lips?"

"Your toes."

"Oh Frank." She turned and threw a pillow at me. "Be serious, won't you?"

"O.K.," I said, "I'll be serious. Magee, I love you."

At that she turned solemn. "That's a four-letter word," she said. "I won't have it in my house."

I felt things changing in me, subterranean shiftings. I worried that I was falling apart; but then doesn't the caterpillar, feeling the shifts that signal the time to leave the cocoon, imagine he is dying too?

A couple of events stand out from this agonizing though relatively quiet period. After dropping Max and Magee off at the airport one afternoon to attend a weekend wedding, I drove morosely back home in the Ocelot. As I turned down Malomar Road, I saw a red Mazda whiz past me as though the streets were on fire behind it. I couldn't see that well, as it was moving so fast, but I had the impression that the entire interior of that small vehicle was draped in bright-colored things—scarves, feather boas, and filled to bursting capacity—although there appeared to be only the single occupant behind the wheel, and no passengers.

I could have sworn the driver was Kitten Caboodle—though as far as I knew, she lived on the other side of the mountains, in Studley City.

That same afternoon there came a nearly frantic call from Henry.

"Where's Max?" he practically shouted into the receiver, once he realized it was me, and not Magee, on the line.

"He's not home," I said.

"Well, tell him to call Henry, goddammit, wouldja?"

"O.K.," I said.

I don't know why, but I never did tell Max to call Henry Goddammit Wouldja that time either.

One morning when Max was away I woke up beside Magee.

Her eyes flicked open and then shut and then open again. She saw me watching her, and smiled. Her lids drooped shut while she groped around the nightstand with one hand. "Cigarette," she mumbled faintly. I reached one out for her—this had become one of my basic functions as a lover—then put it in her mouth and lit it for her. She drew on it without opening her eyes, exhaled with a sigh, and relaxed back onto her pillow.

"This can't go on," she said.

A stab of panic went through me. "*What* can't go on?"

"Life," she replied.

I had to stop myself from sighing with relief.

But she was right, of course. Life couldn't go on like this—it was sheer insanity. And yet, I couldn't pull out. I felt myself being drawn in deeper, deeper. But what could be deeper than this?

Spring had scarcely ended before the heat was on again, like a switched-on oven. It rose from the land in shimmering waves, rippling the air, making the whole scene seem like a thing underwater. The sun blazed and boiled above our heads, indifferent to us all.

I became restless. Nights I drove Malomar Canyon, Mulehauler Drive, the Coast Highway from San Melonica to Point Mojo. I drank a dozen cups of coffee, then drove Malomar Canyon at eighty miles an hour, passing startled Toyotas and Saabs, the abyss of riverbed spreading itself open beside me like . . . *like Magee,* I thought, and I had to fight the impulse to point the car across the edge, through the guard rails and everything, and take the drop.

I drove out to Hollywood and walked the sidewalks, past the hookers and pimps and drug dealers, the homeless people in cardboard condos . . . *poor folks,* I thought, *with no roof over their heads.* And I, living on the charity and grace of others—others I was betraying—imagined I knew how they felt.

"I love Magee Peterson! I love Magee Peterson!" I bayed

maniacally out the window of the hearse, driving up and
down the Boulevard. Nobody batted an eye.

On the marquee of the Hollywood Optic, I spotted a
movie title that seemed familiar: *Service with a Smile*. At first I
couldn't figure it out. But then all at once it came to me. I
couldn't believe it. He'd done it, old West Covina, after all.
It just goes to show: in Los Angeles, anything is possible.

One day I got the notion to head out on the freeway, over
the mountains into the desert, to see the Joshua trees, like in
the song, rediscover nature. But I'd scarcely passed San Melonica, heading east in the hearse, before the endless junc-
tions and interchanges and bypasses began to seem like the
strands of an enormous web, enveloping me, sending me in
circles. Each highway led to more highways, more frontage
roads, more plastic food and gas stations, businesses and
shopping malls, drive-through everythings, motels equipped
with *Famous Miracle Motion Mattresses*. The asphalt went on
forever, rolling out before me but never getting anywhere—
as though a stage crew were erecting sets in front of me,
then dismantling them after I'd passed, and rushing forward
to erect them again.

I must have been hallucinating by this point, but as I was
negotiating a cloverleaf out by St. Bernard, I could swear I
saw a lost, forlorn-looking minotaur, trapped in the green
spot amidst a labyrinth of crisscrossing overpasses.

Finally, as the sun was beginning to set, I hit a blank wall
of greenish-purple smog that swallowed me up. I had to
turn my headlights on to see my way, and even then they

scarcely cut through. I was the only car on the road, as though I'd stumbled into some sort of no-man's-land, like being trapped in a grade-B horror film. Until at last the highway simply looped back on itself, sending me in the direction I'd come. I couldn't find my way out of the godforsaken city.

Maybe there was no way out.

Finally I did escape Los Angeles, briefly, though not by automobile, and not by choice but by necessity. My father was dying again, and I flew back East to see him. I say "again," because by all accounts he'd been dying for at least a decade—but stubborn as he was, he not only refused to cross the threshold in the two weeks I spent there, he rallied enormously. By the time he'd resumed his customary pastime of eyeing the nurses up and down, despite the octopus of tubes emerging from his permanently helpless body, I figured he was good for another year at least, and it was time to go back to California. I'm not sure he knew who he was saying good-bye to; but as he gripped my hand his eyes went wide and very white, and his mouth worked mightily as though he were trying to say something. It never came out.

It was on the plane back to Los Angeles that I finally found the time to read *Oysters in the Storm*. I'd been avoiding it both because I couldn't bear the hype and because I couldn't face Max's eagerness to hear my opinion. I didn't know what would be worse—to have to tell him it was bad, or to have to tell him it was good. I'd put him off as long as I could with the excuse that I was hard at work on my own manuscript. But on the flight from Newark I reluctantly picked it up at last.

To my amazement, it *was* good: a gripping plotline, fantastic characters, inventive ideas—and not a breast in sight. Damned if he didn't do it, I thought. Not that I couldn't do better someday, of course. But his day was now. Still, I must admit the thought rankled a bit. Did Max really have to have Magee, fame, the money and the Ocelot—*and* be the most compelling writer in America?

I sat reading through the first hours of the flight, ignoring the film, refusing the headphones, unmoved by several episodes of turbulence and the crying infant in seat #23A, two rows behind me. I scarcely noticed the snoring of my seatmate, a balding insurance salesman from Seattle. I neglected to visit the bathroom. My only desire was to finish the story before I was interrupted by something inconsequential, like landing or having to pick up my baggage. I became so immersed I even managed to forget it was Max who'd written it.

Then, as the book neared its climax, I came upon the following passage, delivered by the heroine to her lover as she was about to face her ultimate challenge:

> *Do you know how much I love you?*
> *I love you as much as all the salt in all the oceans, as much as all the sand in all the deserts, as much as every ant in every anthill, every blade of grass on every suburban lawn. . . .*

I suddenly recognized not only that segment, but the tone of the entire book.

No wonder it was so easy for me to forget it was Max who had written it.

He hadn't.

I landed in Los Angeles in the middle of another apocalypse. The Santa Ana winds had blown up in my absence—sixty miles an hour, one-hundred-degree temperatures, straight out of the desert—and it seemed all of Southern California was burning. Flying in, I glimpsed smoke rising from a dozen or more fires. Although the pilot assured us there had not yet been much damage to populated areas, the winds showed no sign of abating, and there was no telling what was to come.

Our cabbie picked me up at the airport, and we set off together on the eeriest drive of my life. The wind had strewn sparks and bits of burning debris across such a wide zone that firefighters had no hope of keeping up with it all. Small, localized blazes burned untended in fields and on hillsides along the highway. Smoke rolled up behind the mountains in black, boiling thunderheads. Walls of it blew across the road, like banks of fog, sharp with the scent of burning grasses. There was no way to get any air; no way of escaping the heat and smoke. Sweat ran down my face and seeped along my back, despite the hopeless laboring of the taxi's air conditioner.

Ash rained down on our windshield, while the wind blew

harder and harder, gusts rocking the cab on its axles. We passed a bank temperature readout that said it was 103 degrees. Meanwhile, the freeway was thronged with vehicles, as usual, driving along to wherever it was they were going, as though it were just another ordinary afternoon, as though this happened all the time—and in the Southern California summer, I suppose it did.

Needless to say, I was on fire too. I hadn't seen Magee in weeks, and had hardly eaten or slept. All I could do was dream about her. I'd consoled myself by writing portraits of her, telling myself they would somehow fit into my novel. But at this point, I was ready to burn them. All those months of discussion and anticipation about *Oysters in the Storm*—and it was nothing but an enormous lie. I'd been betrayed by both of them. It may sound odd, but I felt as though I'd been cuckolded.

We passed a body shop; mounted on the roof was an old Lincoln with two front ends, each pointing away from the other, going in two directions at once. I knew exactly how that car felt.

I found Max and Magee both in a foul mood too, tense and simmering. Magee had adopted a new look while I was gone, reminiscent of her punk-artist phase from back at Boscoe. Her hair, clipped to within an inch or two of her scalp, spiked up in red-orange bursts, as though she had begun to ignite. Her eyes were big and luminous, and the way her summer skirt and halter top clung to her body—the body that mere fabric could scarcely contain—I could well believe combustion was possible.

But I tried to divert my mind from such matters. I knew I had to confront Magee first, and alone, about *Oysters*. I couldn't think of any explanation to give either of them for how I had discovered her manuscript; and in my current state, if I confronted them together, I might easily slip up and give away our secret. The ash was coming down too thickly on the patio to sit outside; and so we stayed in the living room, sweating and mopping at our faces, while we went through the motions of reasonable conversation. Magee's eyes kept flicking across to meet mine and I kept avoiding them. She and Max filled me in on what I'd missed—or the external events, at least. I was beginning to realize that they were both rather skilled at leaving out key elements of information. The two of them sat chain-smoking, generating as much smoke inside, it seemed, as there was outside.

After an hour of agony, the phone mercifully rang and Max lumbered off to his study to take the call. As he left the room I noticed his paunch seemed bigger than ever, and his shoulders were bowed, as though some new, great weight had descended on them.

Magee was on her feet and halfway across the room to me when I said: "Magee, how could you do it?"

"Do what?" She stopped, tilting forward on her toes like a dancer halted in mid-step. "What are you talking about?"

"Oysters in . . . the Fucking . . . Storm." I was so furious I could scarcely get the words out.

She stared at me for what seemed like a long time. "So you know too?"

"*Too?* What are you talking about?"

"Frank," she said, "I'll explain this all to you as soon as we get a minute alone. But promise me before Max comes back that you won't mention this to him yet. Things have gotten more complicated than you realize. . . ."

"More complicated than this? Max gets heralded for finding an incredible new voice, and *you* wrote the book? Magee, I can't believe you deceived me——"

"I'm not an ideal, Frank, I'm a woman. A real, live person." She looked at me almost pleadingly. "I told you, I've never wanted my work out in public, where people could drool on it. This way it's just another book of Max's——and they're drooling on him already."

Maybe the sparks I was throwing off were starting to catch, because all of a sudden she added: "Besides, who says I have to tell you everything?"

"Everything?" I couldn't believe what I was hearing. "Everything? This is a pretty big 'everything' to overlook."

Magee's eyes flashed fire. "You don't own me, Frank," she said. "You're just borrowing."

I felt suddenly like Humphrey Bogart, in one of his face-offs with Lauren Bacall.

"Yeah," I snapped back. "And the interest payments are getting a little too high."

I stalked off to my apartment to chill out and take a shower.

O.K., I thought. *Maybe there's some reason for not putting the whole thing on the table yet. I'll wait for her explanation.*

But not too long.

As for Max—well, I'd have to deal with him later.

We retreated to the Malomar Café, out by the pier, to drink beer and watch the spectacle of the fire, amidst the coolness of the air-conditioning and the safety of numbers. Our castle was backed up against the ridge that separated Malomar Road from the Coast Highway, so at home we couldn't see the planes and helicopters struggling to hold the flames back at the top of the higher ridges to the east. Here, with the entire Coast Range visible through the big front windows, we could watch everything.

The place was packed: every table full, locals lined one behind the next on the swivel stools by the counter, TV on over the kitchen door giving up-to-date reports every few minutes. A pair of haggard waitresses ran around trying to attend to everyone. The three of us crammed into a corner on a bench, and pulled over a tree stump that was supposed to be a decoration to use as a table. Everyone seemed to be overlooking the no-smoking rule for the moment— whether because you couldn't control people under these circumstances or because it hardly mattered when the air was filled with smoke already, I wasn't sure. At any rate, our chrome and vinyl surroundings were filled with smoke and noise, as though we were back in the 1950's, and the atmosphere resembled some strange sporting event—although the joviality, I'd have to say, felt a little forced. As for Max, Magee, and I, we all seemed on the point of going for one another's throats. Magee wouldn't meet my eye, Max wouldn't meet hers, and I wouldn't meet Max's, so there we had it: a perfect circle of mutual avoidance.

We sat and talked of disaster, until the red, glaring eye of the sun slid sizzling into the sea. As the light faded we could see an orange glow emerging from beneath the black clouds to the east, as though they were burning coals; as though the entire sky had been set ablaze. Yellow and orange fingers of flame felt their way along the top of the Coast Range, while planes dropped chemical bombs along the ridges, sending up surges of colored light. Helicopters strained skyward with enormous slings dangling beneath them, filled with water from the Malomar Reservoir; they dropped their loads on the flames too, and up came enormous clouds of steam that rolled away and dispersed into the sky.

"It looks like World War Three out there," said Max, to no one in particular, and nobody quarreled with the comparison.

It was strange to just sit there and watch it happen, but as everyone kept saying, no evacuation order had been given, and where would we all go anyway? According to the TV, the blaze had burned all the way down to the highway up north, where the firefighters had stopped even bothering to oppose it, choosing instead to focus their efforts where the risk was greatest. On the highway south, toward the city, the traffic was jammed up for miles, with only more flame and chaos beyond that. There was talk of Malomar being declared a disaster area for the second time that year.

To which Magee's comment was, "*Life* is a disaster area."

I could picture spokes of flame fanning out into the night, through Malomar Canyon, and Doppelganger and Latino Canyons, running like rivers of lava toward the sea. I thought of the people who lived there, gathering up photographs and valuables, children and dogs and cats, and loading them into their automobiles and roaring out ahead of the flames, down-canyon too to the seaside, and I hoped there would be somewhere for them to go. Once again the gymnasium at Saltspray was overflowing with refugees, and the highways were choked with cars full of families looking for a place to spend the night.

"All we need is a set of fiddles to accompany the experience," I managed to quip as we stared upon the spectacle. But I would have made a poor Nero, and no one laughed. There were too many customers, and too much smoke, and the air-conditioning had given up trying to cope long ago. I could feel my shirt sticking wetly against my back, while sweat beaded up on Magee's face and rolled down Max's cheeks in such broad streams they could have diverted it to keep back the flames. Despite her agitation—or maybe because of it—Magee appeared more radiant than ever; her eyes flashed with greenish light, and her entire being glowed, as though lit from within. With a supreme effort I turned my mind—and tried to turn my heart—from her again and again.

Max had just fired up a fresh cigarette—he was already grumbling because the waitress told him he couldn't light a cigar—and suddenly he started coughing and couldn't stop. The coughing fit was tremendous, astounding; he was doubled over gasping for a good ten minutes while the manager and the other customers clustered about, pounding him on the back and forcing him to drink water. His eyes looked wide and startled, as though he were a fish hauled suddenly onto dry land, amazed this could have happened to him.

"Christ," he said, once he'd finally recovered. "You know, smoking ought to be better than it is, for all the trouble it causes you." He sipped at the water someone had handed to him, and picked up a cigarette from the pack in front of him. "Such a small thing . . ." he said, examining it, "and so dangerous!"

"Like black widows," said Magee, lighting one up for herself.

We had another beer, watching while the orange glow grew ever brighter in the sky and the reports on the television became ever more dire, and the café became ever more crowded and claustrophobic. Magee, too, appeared to be growing more and more agitated, until at last she burst out: "What are we all doing? The whole city is about to burn— and we're just sitting here drinking!"

"That seems like a reasonable response to the situation," said Max.

"We should be home packing," she said, "in case we have to get out."

"C'mon, Magee." Max took a sip of his beer. "They're not going to just stand back and let Malomar burn. Northlake Village, maybe. But Malomar?"

"They can't control everything, Max," Magee said. "Things can change any minute. Look at *your* new direction." The words were as spiky as her new hairdo. For a moment there was a palpable charge in the air, like an electric current.

"Listen, Magee." Max leaned forward, his big sweaty body moving beneath his sweat-stained shirt. "They haven't given an evacuation order yet. They're telling us to stay home and keep the highways clear. There's no shortage of water to fight the flames"—he nodded toward the huge Pacific out the window behind us—"and there's the Coast Highway between the hills and us to stop them anyway. We're going to be fine, O.K.?"

"We're always going to be fine, aren't we, Max," said Magee. "The creditors aren't going to take the house. The newspapers aren't going to skewer us from one end to the other. The fire's not going to sweep down those hillsides all the way to the sea—it's all just fictions, right, Max?"

"We're not going to burn, dammit!" Max slammed his fist on the table and started himself off into another round of coughing.

"Max," said Magee, "I'm afraid it's time to Face the Fucking Fire."

Every happy couple may be happy in its own way—but all unhappy couples are alike. At about that point I got up and left. There was too much confusion, too much smoke, no air to be had anywhere. Max and Magee were so involved in shouting at each other they hardly seemed to notice my departure. I'd had enough. I wasn't married to them, was I? And to tell you the truth, I was feeling a bit sick of them both.

Just as I was about to step through the door, someone flipped over the channels on the TV and there on the screen was the professor from that first party, Vern Akler, larger than life—although, as usual, he was missing from the shoulders down. He appeared to be taking part in some kind of panel discussion. I could have sworn as I went out the door that he was saying something like, "Science has just disproved the existence of energy and matter"—but then, I was moving pretty fast, and I might have heard it wrong.

It was eerie out on the beach by myself—skeins of smoke moving across the stars, fires dotted along the dark spine of the Coast Range as far as I could see, and the moon, big and red and round, rising up through it all like an enormous, bloodshot eye. I must have walked for miles that night on the dark, sweltering sand, searching by moonlight for some trace of the hidden alcove, that mysterious hermitage, while the ash rained down on my head like fallout, like the end of the world.

12

In Which Max Takes Me to Hell
and (Not Quite) Back

I STRAGGLED back to the castle, tired and hungry, not knowing where else to go. I'd planned on heading straight up to my apartment—I was through with the love triangle thing, the whole sick scene, and was resolved to pack up my belongings and get out of there. If I couldn't take the hearse, then I'd call our cabbie and have him drive me over to my aunt's house in Trillion Oaks. But as I crossed the driveway I noticed a strange, flickering glow spilling through the open front door of the castle and into the blackness, casting an orange rectangle of light upon the ground. I hesitated, walked on past, then stopped and turned back.

I stepped through the front door to find the place full of flame: candles burning everywhere in the darkened living room, a fire raging in the fireplace; even the countertop burners by the bar were lit. Max stood there, dead drunk, grinning diabolically in the middle of it all.

"Welcome," he slurred, puffing on his cigar, "to Hell!"

Christ, I thought. *He's gone completely off his rocker.*

The place was stifling; the plants were wilting before my eyes.

"Max——" I didn't know what to say or do before the spectacle. "Where's Magee?"

"She's off . . . somewhere," he gestured vaguely. "Doing her own thing. She needs that, you know. . . . We all do." He waved in the direction of the driveway. "She took the Occie."

Magee out driving, I thought, *with the whole city on fire.* I wondered how much she'd had to drink. "But what on earth——"

"We're not on earth anymore, my lad, remember? We're in Hell!" With that Max picked up an unlit tiki torch from several tilted into a corner, thrust it into the fire, and began waving it around the room.

"Max——" I felt the heat flare against my face, and the sharp tang of smoke flooded my nostrils. "Is there some kind of problem here?"

"Problem?" Max brandished the torch like a lunatic warrior. "I'll tell you what the problem is. Problems are the problem, that's the problem!"

Having never been faced with a madman pyromaniac before, I had no idea what to do; but if I left Max to his own devices, it seemed likely he'd send the whole place up in flames. Then I had one of my rare flashes of inspiration.

"In that case, what would you say to getting us both a Jack Daniel's?" I looked at him as calmly as I could. "Then we can sit down and you can tell me all about it."

"Jack Daniel's?" Every demon has his weak point. Max looked back at me for a minute. "O.K., Frankie," he said. "Sure." He lowered the torch.

After casting about for someplace to put it, Max set the thing upright into a vase beside the fireplace. There it continued to flame away, making our shadows dance against the walls like drunken bears.

He fixed us both a Jack Daniel's, spilling half of it on the bar, dropping ice cubes on the floor, crunching them around beneath his feet. Smoke was filling the room; I went around quietly opening the windows and doors.

Max walked up at last and handed me my drink, sloshing a good deal of it onto my hand in the process. Then, cigar in one hand and drink in the other, he looked me unsteadily in the eye and raised his glass in salute.

"Frankie, my lad," he announced, "I'm ruined!"

He drew on his cigar and breathed two long spears of smoke out of his nostrils. I couldn't tell if he looked more like Saint George, or the dragon.

"Ruined? Max, what do you mean?"

"You might say . . . I've been Caboodled."

"What are you talking about?"

"It's Kitten Caboodle—she's bared all!"

"So?" I was genuinely confused. "Isn't that her business?"

"Frankie," said Max, "this is no time for joking. Listen, Caboodle has spilled the beans on the whole thing!"

"You mean she told Magee about your affair?" *Whoops,* I thought—but my unexplained knowledge of the event seemed to go right by him.

"Worse than that. She's telling the world about the *whole* thing!"

"Max, you're not making sense. What whole thing?"

"Oysters in the Storm."

We were at one of those conceptual impasses. I took a deep breath, trying to remain calm. "Max," I said, "what exactly is Kitten Caboodle telling the world about *Oysters in the Storm?*"

"That Magee wrote it."

At this I had to sit down. I made Max sit down too. How was I supposed to play this one? I couldn't let on that I already knew about it, could I? I was feeling more confused than I'd felt during my entire confusing stay at Malomar.

Once Max had settled down I got up, doused the tiki torch, turned off the burners on the countertop, and poured us both a glass of water. Then I made him tell me the story one step at a time.

It seems that Kitten Caboodle, during their tryst, had managed to pocket a key to the house—a not too difficult task, considering Max could never keep track of his keys anyway. She'd slipped in while we were all away, probably that afternoon I'd seen her driving down Malomar Road, after getting the gate code from—well, just about any delivery person in Malomar could have given her the code. And then . . .

"She went into my study, Frankie, and searched through my papers. She found the original manuscript for *Oysters,* in Magee's handwriting. I *knew* someone had been going through my things. I'd thought it was Magee——"

A fresh pang of guilt went over me. But some secrets, I thought, were best kept secret.

"Wait a minute, Max." I was playing dumb, hoping for more clarification. "What do you mean the original manuscript was in Magee's handwriting?"

"Get real, buddy," he said—people in Malomar were always telling me to *get real*—"do you think I could have come up with that 'Prophetic New Voice' crap all on my own?"

"Well." I sipped at my water. "I *did* wonder."

"You know Magee can't stand the glare of celebrity, at least not when it shines on her work——"

"But *you* can."

"Bingo, brother." The light of the fire flickered in his eyes, which looked as big as moons in the semidarkness. "It was the perfect compromise. Get her work out there, get me a new voice—all in one fell swoop."

What was a "fell swoop" anyway? I wondered. I'd never known. "But, Max," I said. "Did you really think you'd get away with it?"

"Why not? I get away with everything else."

I had to let that just go by me. "So Caboodle found Magee's manuscript and——"

"Sold the story to *The National Admirer.*"

"Oh," I said. "Oh boy."

"Why . . . ," he moaned. "Why can't I just stick to one woman?"

"Max," I said. "There *is* only one woman."

He had no idea what I was talking about.

The poor guy, I thought. All his faults had surfaced—and like the earth, he was beginning to crack along them.

"The article hasn't even come out yet, but already Paranoid Studios is threatening to sue me for breach of contract. And that's not all—hey, what is this stuff anyway?" He had stopped in mid-sentence and examined his glass. "It's got no kick to it."

"It's water, Max," I said. "The basic stuff of life. It's good for you."

"Oh," he said, skeptically. He went over to the bar, dumped it out, replaced it with bourbon, and sat down again. "Anyway, my accountant called. My creditors have mounted a lawsuit. He's talking bankruptcy. And Caboodle was so upset when I cut off our affair, she even told that bookstore owner I broke his window, and now *he's* suing me too. Frankie, I'm ruined! Soon everything I've built will be gone!"

"Christ, Max," I said. "What are we going to do?"

"Frankie," said Max. "I'm going crazy. Let's wrestle."

"Wrestle?"

But Max was already on his feet, a crazed light playing about his eyes. "C'mon, Frankie. Didn'tcha ever used to wrestle in high school? It'll be good for us, let out this pent-up aggression. . . . C'mon, bud."

"What pent-up aggression? Max, you're drunk."

He started dancing around the room like some two-bit boxer, his shadow stretching to twice its normal size on the wall. "C'mon, Frankie, what are you, some kind of a wimp?" He pulled his shirt off and circled me; the firelight danced off his belly, which looked enormous, forested with small, dark hairs. "What we really oughta have is loincloths. And some oil, to grease up our bodies——"

"Max——"

"I'm flying, Frank," Max crowed, prancing about the darkened room, taking a few punches in the direction of his shadow. "I'm off my butt! I'm tellin' ya, Frankie——fuck writing. *This* is what I was born to! This! I'm a goddamned drunk!" His eyes were shining with an almost inhuman light. Completely unveiled is what they were; no defenses, entirely exposed. "A drunk! And you know what? I love it. I'm burning up, Frankie! I'm on fire. Feel my hand! Go ahead! Touch me!"

He held out his hand, like a challenge. To humor him, I reached over and touched it. The next thing I knew he had my arm twisted up behind my back, and my whole body was shoved up against the mirrored wall beside the fireplace.

"Frankie, Frankie," Max chanted in my ear, like an overgrown kid, the neighborhood bully. "Where'd you ever get a name like Frankie, anyway?"

"My name's not Frankie, you bastard," I said. "It's Frank!" My face was mushed up against the glass and I could see the room reflected there, distorted and glowing red.

Max was talking straight into my ear. "Oh yeah? And

where do you think Frank comes from? It's short for Francis, isn't it? Now, tell me that's not some kind of pansy name—Francis."

That got me where it hurt. I'd been told I was named for Ben Franklin—but deep down, at bottom, I think that's what I always feared I was: nothing but a Francis.

"So what are you, Frankie? Some kind of fairy? Huh?"

At that my fuse must have finally run out. The next thing I knew I had Max up against the wall, and then he had me down on the floor, and then I wriggled free again. He had the greater weight, but I was faster and more flexible, and the booze had made him slow and sloppy. I was seized by a frenzy of strength, like those parents you read about who can lift a car off their child. All the frustration and rage of the past months—of my entire life, maybe—was blowing out in a single massive detonation. We disengaged for a moment and circled each other in the firelight, panting like madmen, our shadows looming red and black against the walls. I tore my shirt off too—now both of us were stripped to the waist, dripping with sweat.

"O.K., Max," I said. "You want to wrestle? Let's . . . fucking . . . wrestle!" With a roar like a . . . I don't know what—certainly not a Francis—I hurled myself at him. I couldn't tell you exactly what happened after that. He had me in a headlock, then I had him in a half nelson, then I had him in a full nelson—I had him in every kind of nelson I could come up with. With his breath of cigars and Jack Daniel's panting into my face, and the hair that covered his belly and chest and even his shoulders, and the weird glow of the firelight, I felt like I was wrestling with the Devil himself. Finally—I don't know how I managed this, except that I must have been possessed—I got him down on the floor in front of the fire. I was kneeling on his chest and I had him by the neck, and I was pounding him against the floor in a fury.

"You bastard!" I shouted. "I'm going to fucking kill you!"

"Frankie—" Max appeared to be saying. "Frankie!" But the voice was very faint and far away. I looked down and it seemed like he was twice the size I was, as though I was sitting on top of a mountain. I could see his mouth opening and closing, and his body shaking and sounds coming out of him. At first I thought he was laughing, and then I thought he was crying, and then it seemed like he was doing both at once. "Frankie," he was saying, "it's your old pal Max. Remember me?"

I stared down at his face and saw his startled, wide-open eyes; and I came back to myself. I looked up and, reflected in the mirrored wall, saw a Frank I'd never seen before: hair hanging in his eyes, dripping with sweat, stripped to the waist and covered in scratches, sitting on top of . . . Max.

It was a strange moment. But then, all moments are strange. It's just that sometimes you notice it, and sometimes you don't. At that point, I just collapsed. I started laughing, and then *he* started laughing, and his chest and his belly heaved me right off onto the floor. We were both laughing so hard we couldn't stand up or speak, just holding our bellies and laughing maniacally as we lay there, until we were exhausted.

"Oh my God, Max—" I began, then broke out laughing again.

"Frankie, you were like an animal . . . a wild . . ."

"Guppy?" I suggested.

We both burst out laughing again.

"No," said Max, "you were nothing like a guppy."

We lay there breathing for a long time, side by side on our backs, pulling ourselves together.

After a while I heard Max sigh. "So I guess I'll be moving along soon," he said.

"What?" I responded, lazily.

"Getting out of this town. Leaving this place for good."

I rolled over and stared at him in the firelight. "Max, what are you talking about?"

He pushed himself up to a sitting position. "You won the match, didn't you? Survival of the fittest, fittest of the species, the animal kingdom and all that. You're the Alpha Male, aren't you?"

"Max, are you drunk, or what?"

He looked at me tragically, one eyebrow going up and one going down, in an expression I would have found comic if he wasn't so serious.

"Listen, buddy," he said. "I know the deal."

"What deal?"

"You and Magee."

"What?" I sat up then too. "But"—I seemed to be only able to speak in monosyllables—"how?"

Max was reaching slowly, deliberately into his pocket; I found myself watching every move.

"I've been reading your manuscript, buddy." He lifted his key chain out and jingled it. "After all, I've got the keys to your apartment, don't I?"

Max and I stayed up for hours after that, talking. He'd always seemed so solid to me, like an older—if somewhat unreliable—brother. But now I felt as though I was the elder, and it was my job to watch over him.

"It's O.K.," he told me. "I'm all mixed up anyway, aren't I? I need to go find myself or something. Get out. I can always go stay with Henry—"

"Henry?"

"Yeah," he said. "He's pissed off because you never pass along his messages." Max rummaged around, came up with a cigar from one of the end-table drawers, clipped off the end, and lit it.

"Listen, Frankie," he said, puffing away. "I love Magee. But I don't know if I *love* her anymore. You get what I mean?"

I had to admit, I didn't.

"Ah," Max sighed, "what a jerk, what a crazy lunatic God must be to make us this way, knowing how it would all turn out." He pulled at his cigar, exhaling smoke. "I can just see him up there, laughing down on us mortals, splitting his sides over all the trouble he's caused us, like the world's just a giant banana peel he's laid down for us to slip on—and he never tires of the entertainment."

I didn't know what to say to that, except it seemed like the most accurate theology I'd heard all day.

"You know what, Frankie?" Max was in one of the most reflective moods I'd ever seen him.

"What, Max?"

"I've just realized it really *is* all a fiction. There is no such place as Malomar. There's no such person as Max, or Frank, or Magee—"

"Max." I turned and looked at him. "People are *real*. We're not all just characters in some book."

"There you're wrong, Frankie," he said grandly, brandishing his cigar. "All the world's a page—and we are its characters."

I felt a wave of tiredness crash over me. I looked at the clock on the mantelpiece: it read 2:30 A.M.

"Max," I asked, "do you think Magee's all right?"

"Ahh," said Max, "she's O.K. She's just out driving. Or she's got a motel and is sitting up watching old movies. That's what she does when we have one of these knockout fights. Then, mark my words—three, four A.M., she'll roll up the driveway. Magee is like a boomerang. She always comes back."

I wondered what on earth we were all going to say to one another when she did.

We were silent for a bit while Max smoked.

"Max," I said, "what were you two ever doing together in the first place?"

He took the cigar out of his mouth and looked at me. "Frankie," he said, "you don't know a thing about love."

I'd heard the phrase before. But this time, I wasn't so sure he was right.

We must have both drifted off after that, but I woke up just past 4:00 A.M. with Max shaking me by the shoulder. The fire had died out and I was curled up in an armchair; the only light came from a few of the candles that hadn't burned all the way down.

"Frankie, give me the keys to the hearse. I want to go look for Magee after all. She's late. I'm worried about her."

"No, Max." I shook my head to get the cobwebs out. I stood up and pulled the keys out of my pocket. "I'll go."

Max gave me a little shove back against my chest. "It's my job," he said, not unkindly, taking the keys out of my hand. "I'm the one who's married to her, after all."

Whatever that meant.

He went out the door; but as I stood there watching him go, an odd thing happened. I heard a strange cracking noise behind me, and turned to see a dark line beginning to form from the top corner of the mirrored wall. Maybe it was the cooling of the fireplace, or the fresh air coming in through the open doors, I don't know—but as I looked on, the crack fanned out from the corner of the mirror, down and across the surface, like a webwork, or a map of the city, until it looked like the whole room, and I myself, had splintered into fragments. One shard fell with a *plink*! against the floor, and then another.

And then the whole mirror came crashing down.

13

The Conclusion of Our Tale

THE EASTERN sky was beginning to lighten over the hills when a call came in from Max. "Frankie, I found Magee. She's O.K., but listen——there's been trouble." He was out of breath. I could hear Magee's voice in the background, high-pitched and excited. "Frankie," he said, "we're going to have to go away for a while."

"Away?" I repeated. My head was so thick I scarcely knew what he was saying. "But aren't you coming back here first?"

"No . . . (mumbles, mixed in with Magee's voice) . . . easier like this. Write this down, the hearse is in . . ." He gave me the address of a parking garage just off Venison Boulevard. Magee's voice was rising in the background to near-hysterics.

"Max," I said, "what's going on?"

"Listen——" Either he was ignoring my question or he couldn't hear it over Magee's interference. "You're my only *friend. Under the bed there's a shoebox. . . . There's enough to do anything you want—" There was a clatter, as though of the phone being dropped. "Anything you—" and the line went dead.*

I didn't know what to think. I'd had too many surprises by that point to be capable of thinking. I walked back into the living room, scene of our evening's revels. There were empty cups and overflowing ashtrays everywhere, spilling out onto the floor, the sofa, the coffee table. As the morning light broke I could see that everything in the room was covered with a faint patina of ash.

I still don't know why I did what I did next. I searched under the bed and found the box stashed back in the corner. It was stuffed full of fifties and hundreds; there must have been ten thousand dollars, maybe more. I didn't bother to count it. I walked back into the living room and pulled up a chair by the fireplace. One by one I dipped each bill into the fire; then, one by one I dropped them onto the sofa, the throw rugs, the base of the curtains, the trash bins. . . .

Just burn it, I thought. This house. It was bound to burn anyway. In fact, it was burning already.

That's the way it happened—in my novel, at least.

But that's not the way it really happened. Things aren't, generally, as dramatic as that in real life. Or as tidy. Although there were ways in which the truth did link up with the fiction.

What actually happened was this:

A half hour after Max left, Magee showed up in the

Ocelot, just like Max said she would, only a little behind schedule. I never did find out what she'd been doing. Maybe she was out driving the freeways, like I'd done, and discovering there was no escape.

"Magee——" I went out to the Ocelot to meet her. "Listen, Max just——"

"I know all about Max," she said through the open window.

Something in her tone made me cautious. "What do you mean?" I said.

She looked at me.

"I found his journals."

"Oh," I said. "Shit."

"Shit is right," said Magee. "One Hundred Varieties of it."

"He went out searching for you."

"He'll be back." She gave me a funny up and down glance. "What happened to your shirt? And why are you so scratched up?"

We didn't go after him. It was too absurd and complicated and dangerous, with the fires burning all over the place——and after all, he was just as likely to show up here as anywhere.

Amidst the uproar, we'd lost track of the radio and TV reports long ago. Maybe they did send someone down Malomar Road with a megaphone like they do in the movies, shouting "Evacuate!" If so, we were too far up the hill, or too tired, or too distracted to hear. Then again, maybe Magee and I were so hungry for each other after two weeks of separation that we ignored the fact that Max might show up at any minute, flung caution to the Santa Ana winds, and tumbled together into my bed, from which an earthquake would hardly have roused us.

Just before dawn Magee drew my attention to a flickering light that rose and fell against the walls. I stepped over to the back window of my apartment just in time to see the first fingers of flame slap themselves over the top of our ridge; then the whole body of the fire came, with the wind behind it.

We had just enough time to throw on our clothes and let the dogs out of the kennels to fend for themselves. Max was off in the hearse, and there was only the Ocelot, with its tiny backseat, into which they would never fit—and even if one of them could, how could we bring ourselves to decide which? The cats, near as we could tell in the brief instant we had to look for them, had fled already; in any case, we figured they each had five or six lives left in their quota, which was more than we could say for the two of us. We grabbed my wallet and Magee's purse, leapt into the Ocelot, and floored it out of there.

A moment later, like characters in some film, we found ourselves speeding down Malomar Road and into the dawn, with fires burning on every side, and no idea where we were headed—only knowing for certain that everything behind us was gone.

"Frank," Magee said, "what are we going to do?"

"I don't know." I really didn't. I don't think I've ever felt so blank in all my life.

We were silent for a moment. "Do you think Max is all right?" I asked.

"Max will always be all right . . ." said Magee, "until he's *not* all right anymore." This was one of those Magee moments, when I had no idea what she meant. She opened her purse and dug around for a cigarette.

"Magee," I asked, "when you took up with me, you didn't know a thing about Max's affairs, did you?"

She shook her head, and lit up a crumpled Chesterfield.

"As far as you were concerned, everything was fine. Why on earth did you do it?"

Magee blew smoke out her window, the end of her cigarette glowing red in the early light. The hint of a smile crossed her face. "I read your manuscript," she said. "No one ever wrote about me like *that* before."

She laughed. We both laughed. Then she collapsed into one of her coughing fits.

Christ, I thought. *Everyone's read the damn book.*

In our little corner of the world, it qualified as a bona fide best-seller.

Epilogue

The rest worked itself out with the inevitability you'd expect from a Greek drama—as though it couldn't have happened any other way. Maybe that's an illusion; but as Magee always says, "What's wrong with a little illusion?"

I've often thought, in the months that have passed since that night of the fires, of one of the more reflective passages I read in Max's journals:

> *Perhaps our agonies are not truly that important. And yet we cling to them—indeed, wear them like life jackets, as though they were the only thing that could keep us afloat on the stormy sea of passion. . . .*

It's classic Max, isn't it? Overwrought, it's true, but it seems to capture what was best in him—that bighearted, almost charming confidence in his own talent, and the idea that through it, maybe, he was somehow doing good. . . .

So, we'd all ended up deceiving each other. Maybe that's just what people are like, I don't know. I'll have to think that one over a few more years.

I guess it all doesn't seem so cut and dried to me anymore. Good and bad, right and wrong, truth and fiction. Life is a greased pig; the more you try to pin it down, the more it gets away from you.

But there was something perfect about Max—if only that he was immaculately and perfectly himself. He wasn't going anywhere, for he'd already arrived. In a way, I suppose, he was a Finished Man.

My life had been narrow before I entered theirs. My self had seemed a small room, stuffy, in which the smells of the world hung too thickly, sounds could not be escaped, and the door was hopelessly jammed shut. My time in Malomar, simply put, made a man of me.

In countless ways, I owe Max a tremendous debt.

I try to turn my mind away from what he might have done if things had worked out differently. If *he* had worked out differently. But after all, he was who he was, like we all are—what more can one say? As Magee puts it: "He was, always and forever, just Max."

We, all of us, have to make a choice. Magee and I, in the end, chose life. And Max?

One night, not long after the last of the fires were extinguished, Max was out on one of his binges, driving the Trojan Hearse. There was no particular drama to the event: he took a curve on the Coast Highway too sharply, and simply went over the edge—a destination that, after all, he'd been aiming at for quite some time.

Voice of a Generation Silenced Forever

read August Snipe's headline in the *LA Times*.

Ghost Writer Still Stalks Point Doom

went the headline in *The National Admirer*.

The effect on his sales was, predictably, enormous. All of his titles immediately hit the best-seller list again—along with Magee's, which was eventually reissued under her name; although she kept the title, *Oysters in the Storm,* as an homage to Max.

Since then she's written another. And another. Magee's *Sea Wrack Diaries* have passed the two million mark for individual sales, making her the millionaire Max never exactly was in life.

She seems satisfied, for once, after all. Maybe she'll end up being the first really happy rich person I know.

After Max died we moved back East, leaving the dream and nightmare of California behind. Maybe we were both built to live in the real world, after all. Max and Magee had never really seemed to fit out West, either one of them. And me? I've never been sure I fit anywhere. Though I seem to be fitting a lot better these days.

We found the dogs after the fires, locked up in the pound with every other harebrained beast that got loose that night and managed to survive. We even rented a van to take them back East with us. They continue to occupy a large place—this is no exaggeration—in our lives.

Magee has discovered aerobics—and after several anguished, angst-filled months in which she chewed her fingernails down to the cuticles, she gave up smoking. I got my meditation practice together; she rededicated herself to the piano. She rarely misses a meeting of her Narcissists Anonymous support group. We've just discovered that she's pregnant.

Love, as Max always said, is the only adventure in the modern world.

And I'm learning to tell the truth. I really am. Well, most of the time.

"Change is always possible," says Magee.

"But you know what?" she adds. "I miss Max."

So do I.

Sometimes I wonder. I ask Magee: "What if Max hadn't—what if he didn't turn out to . . . what if—"

"Frank," says Magee, smiling, putting her hand on my shoulder as I sit working on my manuscript—my new one, of course, for the old one was lost in the fire.

"Frank," she says, "you don't know a thing about love."

We saw not too long ago on the news that the Malomar Rock finally fell, more than a year after the original crisis. It wasn't as bad, somehow, as everyone feared. It took out a lamppost and the corner of a garage, and vanished into the sea.

We heard through the grapevine that our cabbie married Kitten Caboodle.

My father is still hanging on, bed-bound, hooked to feeding tubes, breathing tubes, every kind of tube you could imagine. Whenever he's asked if he'd like to approve a "do not resuscitate" form, he shakes his head no. He seems to like it this way. All of his needs are taken care of, all day long. He doesn't have to do a thing.

God, as far as anyone knows, is still up there, splitting His sides over us.

In a dream, I finally found the secret alcove. I was walking down the beach toward sunset, when something—the flap of a pelican's wing or a pebble tumbling from above—made me look up. Gleaming from a shadowy recess I saw a glint of light that ought not to have been there. I scrambled up the slope, rocks shifting beneath my feet, gravel sliding, falling a foot back for every few feet forward, until, mounting the outcrop, I pulled myself onto a narrow stone shelf.

There it was, set like a jewel into the face of the cliff, equally invisible from above and below. I could see the blue of sky and sea reflected in its windows, the sun's glare reflecting from the glass so brightly I had to shield my eyes. As my vision cleared, I found a weathered wooden facing and a single window made of rectangular panes, separated by unfinished strips. The unpainted door creaked as I pushed it open; dust had settled on the wooden bench by the window; mice had made nests in the narrow bunk. But there, on the bookshelf, I found it all: the great works of literature from throughout the ages. *The Odyssey, The Iliad,* Milton and Shakespeare, Joyce's *Ulysses,* Dante and Cervantes.

Beneath these, on the table, was a handwritten manuscript: the final testament left to the world by the self-liberated hermit who'd lived here. But when I opened its cover, dust rising and glittering in the light, I found the text was gibberish: letters pushed together at random, punctuation marks inserted in the center of words, numbers shoehorned between the letters. I looked up to see the sun about to set, its gold and crimson glow spreading over the water. I wanted to take the manuscript with me, to sort out whatever code it was written in, but I could not lift it. When I persisted in trying, it crumbled in my hands. I had to use the last of the remaining light to make my way down the cliff.

I knew I would never find this place again.

The day before we left Malomar, I went for a walk by myself out on the beach. I thought I saw old Bobby Zipperman, walking far and away down the sand, at the base of the cliffs where the alcove was said to be hidden.

But it might not have been him at all.

About the Author

A Zen practitioner for the past fifteen years, Sean Murphy is also the author of *One Bird, One Stone: 108 American Zen Stories,* a chronicle of Zen practice in the West, as well as a Hemingway Award–winning first novel *The Hope Valley Hubcap King.* He has produced and directed documentary films, founded a theatre company, and performed as a songwriter and guitarist. He teaches writing seminars in the U.S. and abroad, and teaches writing, literature, and film at the University of New Mexico. He lives with his wife, Tania, in northern New Mexico. Visit his website at http://www.murphyzen.com.